IN LIMBO

My heart went out to my wife. I don't know that I ever loved her more than I did right that second. I was filled with a deep, painful yearning, a giving kind of love that was different in uncanny ways than any I'd ever felt for anyone. A love which contained elements of fresh wisdom, I think, a kind new to me; fragments of wan wistfulness, yes, and a searing regret that I'd never been a better man. She'd deserved the best.

Smiling, I put my arms around her.

"God," she said softly, flinching away, "it's *cold* in here."

Her comment did not immediately register, however. I was watching the way my arms, as I reached for her, passed directly through the suntanned skin of her bare back, and seemed to enfold nothing but my own, wanting body.

I hadn't touched her at all. I couldn't.

I could not touch my own wife!

I shrieked then. It was a lot more than screaming, it had terror and supplication in it. I shrieked; then I shrieked again.

But she didn't hear.

A mistake. I said that aloud. *Some awful mistake has been made. There's no way it's the way it looks.*

Yet, sweet heaven, the question was certainly inescapable: *what if I am dead?*

I knew then that if being haunted was frightening, haunting was a much worse thing. It was the worst fate that could befall anyone . . .

Leisure Books
By J.N. Williamson:

PROFITS
THE TULPA
THE LONGEST NIGHT
PREMONITION
PLAYMATES
WARDS OF ARMAGEDDON (with John Maclay)
BROTHERKIND
THE RITUAL
QUEEN OF HELL
THE OFFSPRING
EVIL OFFSPRING

GHOST

J. N. Williamson

*"Sometimes within the brain's old ghostly house,
  I hear, far off, at some forgotten door,
A music and an eerie faint carouse,
  And stir of echoes down the creaking floor."*
—Archibald MacLeish

"There must be ghosts all over the world."
—Henrik Ibsen

DEDICATION

This book, accompanied by my warmest affection and respect, is meant for Mary, my wife and eternal confidante; James Kisner, Mort Castle, Thomas Millstead, and John Maclay; for Ruby Powell, and Darren Harrison, whose talent must be discovered soon; and for my children.

ACKNOWLEDGEMENT

The uplifting final portion of Ghost would have been very different, indeed, without the generous, almost casual suggestions of a highly imaginative writer, Ronald C. Duncan. The little brother I never had, Ron refused to share authorship with me, but he won't prevent me from stressing, in this fashion, his wonderfully innovative ideas or his constant kindness.

Book Margins, Inc.

A BMI Edition

Published by special arrangement with Dorchester Publishing Co., Inc.

If you purchased this book without a cover you should be aware that this book is stolen property. It was reported as "unsold and destroyed" to the publisher and neither the author nor the publisher has received any payment for this "stripped book."

Copyright © MCMLXXXIV by J.N. Williamson

All rights reserved. No part of this book may be reproduced or transmitted in any form or by any electronic or mechanical means, including photocopying, recording or by any information storage and retrieval system, without the written permission of the Publisher, except where permitted by law.

Printed in the United States of America.

GHOST

"Somewhere—in desolate, wind-swept space—
    In twilight-land—in No-man's land—
Two hurrying Shapes met face to face,
    And bade each other stand.

'And who are you?' cried one, agape,
    Shuddering in the gloaming light.
'I know not,' moaned the other shape,
    'I only died last night.'"
—*Identity* by T. B. Aldrich

"No more fiendish punishment could be devised, were such a thing physically possible, than that one should be turned loose in society and remain absolutely unnoticed by all the members thereof."

—*Psychology* by William James

CHAPTER 1

I awakened this morning and again found I was completely incapable of rising. It is a condition which, by now, provides no cause for further alarm. One can get used to just about anything, I suppose. And after all, it's been this way for—well, for a considerable period of time. *(Weeks? Months?)* I have access neither to newspapers nor to any calendar; no television set or radio was installed here. That is why I really have no clear idea how long I've been . . . wherever this is.

I know I am in absolute darkness, total isolation.

By these seemingly courageous admissions it should not be assumed that I was always sanguine about my plight. I am, after all, a man who's been reasonably active. Not that slightly annoying fellow who makes you feel guilty by insisting upon jogging even in snow or playing three sparkling sets of tennis in driving rain, but still and all, active enough. And so I have not enjoyed being trapped, or immobilized.

Frankly, it scared hell out of me at first.

In fact, there was a time when I'd regained consciousness and peered about me in this consuming ever-night, and I screamed for help. I admit that. Yes, I do; I'm not even ashamed. I screamed my lungs out for someone to come to my aid, *anyone*.

They didn't.

Do you have any idea what it's like to find yourself, without explanation, in a literally intolerable situation and be able to do nothing about it? Yes, we claim that this and that set of circumstances is intolerable. But see that word for a minute, consider its meaning. Because it means you *cannot* tolerate it.

That's when, like me, you find out you can. Now I begin to wonder an entire range of dreadful things, some of them sheerly terrifying. What, for example, if I am somewhere that my loved ones postively cannot follow? There are such places, remember. A hospital infirmary, a jail, if people wanted to get hardnosed about things. How could Louise even begin to persuade them to let her in?

But perhaps it's worse. Perhaps some comedy of errors has caught me up in a mistake, placed me in the hands of the CIA, or the KGB. Such things happen. They do. I've read about them, never shuddering really, even smiling, turning the page. But what would you do if some agency identified merely by several mysterious letters thought *you* were someone else? And what would *they* do about it? Would they put a person in here to rot?

I imagine I am ill. That Louise and others actually know where I am, what's wrong with me. It's become easy to conceive a wide range of plausible explanations, since I'm a writer. For example, let's suppose some hideous science-fiction thing happened and I have been . . . *replaced*. Replaced by someone, something, pretending to be Zachary Edson Doyle. And he/it has my memories, and all my identification, sits at my place in the front room or, worse, sleeps in my bed. With Louise. And what if—my imagination conjures this one up now that I'm already scared silly —*what if I am dead?*

I sound like a crazy person to myself. Absence of light, of the human face, will do that. But it doesn't matter if I talk aloud this way, because I certainly seem to be hopelessly alone.

Okay, there may be many rational explanations to fit the facts. Madness is one of them, undeniably. I was under a lot of pressure after my new book met with sharply critical comment, or no comment at all. That always makes me feel invisible anyway. Creative types always feel invisible when nobody notices them, or cares. Hence—or is it thence?—it's not entirely beyond the realm of possibility that, in the conscious mind, I simply went bonkers. Flipped out; cracked up; blew my lid.

The scenario of how I lost my sanity isn't actually hard to imagine.

Let's say I went out to the loft over the garage which I converted, two years ago, to a sort of working den. I'm tired out, waiting for a royalty check to come in so Louise and I can take our annual vacation, that annual vacation we haven't taken, because of various pressures, for three years. The mail brought nothing but bills. Now (my theory for going bonkers reads) the ideas aren't coming. I try all day, work half the night. Zilch. Nothing on the page in the typewriter but the good old brown fox jumping the lazy dog again—and that's when I go crackers. I destroy the den, perhaps, and leap down the flight of stairs to the garage floor. Louise finds me there an hour later. This is where the scenario slows down, because I don't know whether to imagine Louise found me with a hose from the automobile exhaust pipe stuck in my yap like an all-death sucker, or if I struck my head upon the cement floor and went blind.

Why do we say we 'lost' our sanity? Surely it's *taken*. No one could possibly be so careless as to misplace something so precious.

As theory, blindness has elements worth reflection. I can't see anything here. Unfortunately, however, it does not explain why I can't even sit up. I've heard of the "press of responsibility" but I doubt its weight is sufficient to pin me down for countless days on end.

I'm thinking blindness over, though. (Here, parenthetically—editors never like parentheses, you know, because they quite rightly find them self-indulgent; they tend to consist of the author's wholly unsought opinions and views—let me note, *open* paren, that I am pretty much winging it by talking aloud like this most of the day, because nobody seems to object and it's better to have my own company than nobody's, *close* paren.) As a *possibility:* blindness. You see, like most of us I've spent many a night in rooms that were dark, really dark. The kind where one drags out the hand-before-the-face cliche and tries to hum a little fresh emphasis into it.

The first night of my honeymoon with Louise, for example. That was *really* dark. At that time she was a modest little mouse of a thing who honestly believed that her tummy was a turn-off because of stretchmarks from Eddie, the kid from her previous marriage. She told me, as bluntly as possible considering the way she sat there in her slip on the edge of the bed wailing, that she absolutely could *not* consummate our marriage unless we left the lights off. And when I agreed, trying to win the award for Mr. Considerate of the Year, it looked like a damn coal mine inside that motel room!

It was neon lights on 42nd Street in Manhattan in comparison to this.

I am able, you see, to get my hand before my face— just barely—and I can't, I really can't, see my fingers. When I put my arm up as far as I can stretch it, I have the sensation there's *something* there, just out of reach. Sometimes I think it's an oxygen tent, although why that would be beneficial for a newly blinded man I have no idea. The point I'm trying to make is simple:

It's so goddam *dark* in here that there are times when I think I'm going mad, if I haven't already.

Easy, Old Zach; easy does it. I sigh, willing my legs to reach as far down as they can; and even that happens to be an enigma for me, because I can't get any *sensation* in the old gams anymore. I don't really know if they're moving or not. Jesus, what a frigging mess I've turned out to be! A crazy, blinded paraplegic who is also damned near deaf.

That one, qualified the way it is, makes me feel better. Microscopically. (Microscopically? God, could I be *shrinking*, the way Richard Matheson's character did?) I'm being firm, trying to concentrate; and while the sound is at a distance, every now and then it does weakly reach my ears. Maddeningly. There are, you see, such noises and they could actually be other people, conversing. Real, honest-to-God, *human people;* and they have this tender, soft, sort of lifeless tone to their voices. *If* they are voices. Then, too, sometimes I hear what could be automobile horns blowing and the distant, eerie wail of sirens.

I gotta admit it, much of this is eerie that way; weird. Often. It is a feeling of being an unnoticed, tacked-on, needless part of existence with the inability to experience much of anything. It is a . . .

What if I am dead?

Lord, oh Lord, why did *that* thought come back? Strike it! Get out the old Liquid Paper and spread it generously around. It never happened.

I really thought I'd successfully forbidden that idea to return. Because it cannot be true, it must now, *it really must not.*

Here is what I actually believe. This is my genuine, definite, favorite theory of what has happened: I am in a hospital bed, under virtually constant sedation. One of the newer, still largely experimental drugs has been given me. Now the consciousness that I *think* I am experiencing is like those poor souls who believe they have "died" under surgery, on the operating table, and are on their way to heaven. Delusion, see?

Except my eyes are closed, according to this pet

theory. That's why I think it's dark, rather than godly light at the end of the mystical old tunnel. Why, this could even be hysterical blindness! Sure. Sure! That would account for why it is so unbelievably . . .

Uh-uh. Strike "unbelievably," because it's happening to me, all right. It's going on, for real, and I must face facts. This is HAPPENING; THIS is *REAL*. Because I think that's really lovely, in a crazy fashion. It means that one of these days I will surely awaken. I'll open my eyes, and *see*. I'll raise my head a bit, look around and then my sweet pretty Louise will be looking down at me with tears of relief in her eyes, and her wonderful Only-Louise smile; and she will say, softly and tenderly; "Welcome back, tiger . . ."

Oh, dear God, how I want to hear those words, that corny message. *Welcome back, tiger!* If only someone would say that to me, right now—just once—all this would be rendered unimportant. It would come together like a silly cloud of sinister black smoke and *poof!*—disappearance! "Welcome back, Zach, you so-and-so—*welcome back!*"

Even if they would penetrate this thick lump of a skull of mine—with hypnosis, maybe?—and explain it all to me: "It's this way, Mr. Doyle, thirty-eight year old midwest author, decent human being. You are a very sick guy but we feel pretty sure we can save you. Okay? We know it is dark in this room, but that's for your own good, all right? We're in and out, all the time; you aren't really alone. There are doctors and nurses and neurosurgeons up the poopshoot, trying hard as the devil to figure out how long your hospitalization will last—*ha, ha,*—and feeding you intravenously. Why, Louise has been by your side right along, Zach Doyle. Both Eddie and your own son Tommy drop round regularly; there are drawings they made at school—homemade Get Well Quick cards—standing now on your dresser, right by your bed. So don't worry. Your blindness and immobility aren't permanent, you aren't insane, you're not in jail, and the CIA and Mafia didn't really grab you."

You're dead, *that's all it is.*

Shit! Shit, shit, SHIT! Dear Jesus, why can't I shake that miserable notion out of my head?

And why won't somebody come to rescue me from this awful, dark, quiet place?

CHAPTER 2

"It's all no more than a terrible blunder, of course, and I think it's essentially pointless to establish blame. Don't you?"

The heavyset being turned with lethargic grace to peer, from beneath hooded lids, at the figure who had addressed him. Like it or not, the damnable fellow certainly stayed fit, or appeared to. He seemed as dapper, thin, and alert as he had at any previous encounter of the past three thousand years.

It was in the wiry man's office that they'd met, and Chauncey Wells added an additional thought to his hasty inspection of Newton Link—or the vibrational construct which Link, in after-death, conveyed. He was just as clever and deceptive as ever. Of course, Wells hadn't known the fellow in life; to be fair about it, it was possible Link had sacrificed as much as he had, himself.

Rather than any obsequiousness on his part, it had been the stout Wells' turn to travel. While he loathed physical activity, he believed that the change of climate did his spirit a lot of good. *I am a thin man, too, but disguised,* Wells informed himself. *I'm full of consuming deeds and unangelic cunning and I am blessed with a quickness of thought the competition finds off-putting.* Before replying, he smiled. Of all the self-praising words, a single one really described him: cunning. Basically, that was the only reason that the Company regarded him as a match for the dapper Newton Link. It was why they kept countering with him, century after century.

"Per agreement," he said aloud, blinking, "it was definitely your side's turn to keep an accurate record of those who were departing. You can't deny that." He smoothed his pudgy, pink hands over his snow-white trousers as if washing them of further responsibility. "Unless you've devised some fresh argument I'm not acquainted with."

"Oh, I have, certainly," said the dapper coordinator of departure statistics. His infamous heartiness, possibly his finest disguise in life or in after-death, moved his cold lips in a smirk. "You didn't think I'd let Corporate down at this late date, did you?"

Wells sighed, looking unhappy. "One could at least hope. What have you found?"

"Your oversight, old man. You forgot the periodical mathematical anomalies which unfailingly arise when we have to handle and process figures of this astronomic variety! Hoentgen's curve, to cite one viable statistical-lapse factor. The poly-nuclear nature of such death-digits raised to the tenth power." Link spread his own hands in a gesture of appeal to reason. "The fact that neither Company made conclusive recommendation regarding the man's eventual destination is no more than the fault of recurring anomalies beyond the extrapolative skills of this model computer."

The second being, who once was distinguished but always-overfed Chauncey Wells, scowled and almost shoved himself to his feet. Instead, he sank heavily against the back of his chair, which protested with a discernible squeak. "Yet the fact remains, sir, that there has still been no disposition made for the late American named Zachary Doyle. Surely, you share my shame, Link! It would be bad enough—consider for a moment the inherent trauma to the spirit we both seek, and whether he is still a credit to either Company—but when you've factored in the mathematically certain likelihood that his entire situation is exacerbated—multiplied a thousandfold, day in and day out, until the gentleman receives direction—we have something urgently important on our hands."

"It is serious, yes." Newton Link, at a glance, looked handsome as all hell, with his high-elevation styling of the ebon hair and a three-piece Western-style suit (presumably tailored for him; the climate encouraged vocations demanding heat). Link's gaze shifted from a portrait Wells identified as the Marquis DeSade and his steaming eyes burned into Wells' small ones. "But none of this, my dear fellow, is without precedent. Bear it in mind."

"Oh, that," sighed Wells, faintly coloring.

"Yes, brother Wells, *that*—if you aren't so senile you can't remember back a couple of thousand years." Link shook his handsome head. "I have no wish to step on any toes, especially tenderly religious ones. But do you have the slightest notion of what overlooking the Hoentgen curve did to statistical probability research analysis when—when *that Man* was permitted to rise from the dead?"

"Hoentgen hadn't even died, back then," Wells argued with a ponderous flourish of his meaty hand. "He hadn't even been *born!*"

"That's specious reasoning, sir, and you know it! With any post-life appreciation of fundamental facts, including the overview both our Corporate Presidents take as their natural and inherent right, arguing from the living's viewpoint of time as ongoing instead of constant, it's perfectly clear that a precedent was established for the years ahead."

"I'd hardly compare *Him* with the human Zachary Doyle." Wells snapped it out, then folded his sausage fingers and ruminated. He wasn't about to apologize, regardless of affixing blame. From Wells' standpoint, the anomaly Link alluded to topped all the loving sacrifices, acts of heroism, and sentimental gestures of affection which had been both predictable and allowable. Slowly, he took a look at the renovation that had gone on down there as a consequence of a growing set of arrival figures, and gave Newton Link a mental A for taste. Done in crimson and black, the effect might have been garish, even egocentric, in the hands of a lesser administrator in Link's Company. The new color scheme and vaster office had been earned by the damned fellow's uncanny gift for recruitment. Since that Viet Nam war, on earth, he'd succeeded in achieving a high level of control over nearly a third of the western world—and Link seldom left his desk, even more rarely made sales calls.

The unholy computers, however, were everywhere in Hell now and Link even had one—apparently his favorite toy, judging by the way he kept stroking the filthy thing—at the edge of his wide executive desk.

He decided to bait Link. "You have to give it this much, Newton, if I do say so." He looked back at the dapper devil, his gaze steady. "What happened two thousand years ago may or may not have disrupted old, evil Mr. Hoentgen, but its effects were certainly good for civilization as a whole."

"I don't have to concede any such point!" snapped Link, paling. "Frankly, Wells, I think it is exceedingly bad form to come bustling into my office like a pregnant turtle and trying to heat up all the old debates! Nothing could be resolved between our two Companies then, and nothing can be resolved now."

"But if—"

"No buts! Our position remains firm that it was a basic, completely unpredictable statistical malfunction which permitted Resurrection, and, while we never put it in writing, that we're sure your organization's Head intentionally, and with benediction aforethought, interfered with that death." Link hesitated, looking prim as he folded his arms. "And if He *did* tamper, old soul, you people could have the elementary gumption to confess it was a serious breach of contract."

Wells ignored the countering argument. Appearing idle, he prodded the gleaming desktop computer with a fat index. "New toy?" Surely he was meant to see it; when he'd entered, its lights were the only ones in the office and they'd created a certain haloing effect, presumably to earn his approval. Now, with Newton Link practically hugging the thing to his heartless chest, the computer seemed all but ready for hellish enshrinement—along with their impressive display of weaponry, bomb casings, poisons, nooses, and assorted seditious writings.

"I think it will be valuable in my work, yes," Link confessed. Somewhat mollified by the change in subject and attitude on the part of his opposite number, Link tilted back his comfortable executive chair, gesturing urbanely. "Some knowledgable chaps came down from one of those American firms—IBL, or one of those ludicrous acronyms—and they were so good, they even showed the Head a few things." He smiled and his teeth, Wells noted, were no longer perfect. He'd require more time in Vibrational Freeflow or start looking like a grinning shark. "You know, we can always find uses for those computer types."

"Really?" Wells threw up his chubby hands and chuckled. "We won't touch the bleeders ourselves. All that programming, and software, those tubes and relays—well, it's not so much that they destroy their souls as it is that they tend to dehumanize themselves. But don't let me talk shop!" He leaned forward, the chair beneath him squealing. "The thing is, old man, I don't believe we can delay. It isn't right, you know, and it does traumatize the spirit frightfully, as I remarked. It's our position that we need to reach a decision about Zachary Doyle *now*. *Today*."

"It isn't 'right,' you say?" Link lifted a slim finger in warning. "Don't you *dare* try to get around me with that old cliche about 'Christian compassion,' Wells. Not in *my* bailiwick!"

"Nothing of the sort," the fat being murmured innocently. His eyes vanished when he smiled. That instant he might have persuaded any other soul in after-death to consider him a big, bland, affable pussycat. "There's a great deal to be said in your favor, sir; 'balance of power' and all that. No, my good fellow, I had . . . something else in mind."

"Really." Guarded, the dapper host poured a cup of coffee from his service and his hard eyes watched Wells above the rim. "Careful with this. It might be a trifle too hot for your simple taste." He took a sip of his own coffee, and beamed. "Perfectly scalding."

Chauncey Wells blew noisily on his before testing it. When he did, he couldn't resist a smile of admiration. "Ah, those Cuban rascals know their business!" Then he had an idea and stopped with his cup midway to the saucer. "You don't, perchance, have access to, ah, Havana *cigars*?"

Newton Link lifted his own cup. "It isn't our fault if you subsist on a diet of woolly lambs and milk, Wells. Get on with your proposal, I don't have all day."

"*Au contraire*, sir," Wells said, smiling, "but I shan't cavil." He put down his cup, planted his enormous palms on his knees, and leaned across the desk until his face was a foot from Link's. "Does the term *Second Coming* hold any particular significance to you, sir? Think about it a moment, eh? Bestir those aging memory cells, my dear fellow. '*Sec-ond Coming*' . . ."

His first use of the term would have been sufficient. Link slopped half his coffee on the top of his desk but did nothing about it. Beneath his perpetually ruddy complexion, the vibrational rearrangement was angel-white. "You *wouldn't!*" he exclaimed, genuinely horrified. "You wouldn't take low advantage of a situation not of your making—a mere mechanical aberration, no more—to *re-introduce*—"

"*I* wouldn't, of course," Wells said cheerily, shrugging. "But I am the helpless instrument of a far greater apparatus, sir, a mere messenger, if it comes down to that. I have no choice but to do what I am told." He downed the rest of his coffee in a gulp, and grinned happily. "As I recall, that's the sort of argument you people have always held close to your heart. Vertical buck-passing, and all that?"

"You're bluffing!" Link hissed. "Zachary Doyle is just—"

"—Is just *there*," interjected Chauncey Wells, "a decent enough sort, impervious to physical harm, able to materialize or dematerialize if I snap my fingers, *bound* to appear postively miraculous with just a dash of constructive prompting. Of course," Wells added, his eyes opening wide, "if Doyle isn't the man for the job, there is an abundance of those at my place who *incessantly* argue that it's time for—what shall I call it? —the 'real thing'? My vote weighs rather heavily, if I may add as much without seeming unduly immodest."

Now the pallor of Newton Link's apparent skin was replaced by an inching, creeping scarlet that began crawling up the back of his stiff neck and into his fleshless cheeks. "Perhaps we can let Doyle go up. Obviously, I'll have to check it out and that will take a little time. All of Corporate is in the Kremlin for a fortnight." He paused, then raised a brow. "But I see you already know that. My compliments on your intelligence."

Now Wells frowned. "And *I* see you already knew that I know. A neat stall, sir, but insufficient." His fingernail clicked against the glossy computer atop Link's desk. "Just as I am not deceived by the function of this dark instrument. You put it in full view, expecting me to believe it is scheduled for other uses; but I rather imagine one brisk command from you will do the trick." Wells' smile was humorless. "We all have to be prepared for arising challenges more efficiently than before, correct?"

Link glared at him. "You're a clever devil."

"Ah-ah-*ah*," Wells demurred. "My Head disapproves of covert enlistment policies." He patted Link's immaculate cuff. "You've never believed greatly in free choice, have you? None of you chaps understand the principle, or the degree of commitment, of devotion, when a selection has been voluntarily accomplished. But that, you see, is all I'm after—for the time being. That Zachary Edson Doyle's immortal spirit be allowed to return to the house in which he lived. Call it a grade-B haunting for the moment, all right?"

The wiry figure behind the desk shifted uncomfortably. "That sounds too good to be true."

"Correction." Wells raised a fat index. "If it's true enough, it's bound to be good."

"And if I accede to your request? Not to be gauche, but what's in it for us?"

"Opportunity, dear old friend." Wells beamed expansively. "We even give *you* people a chance. But the choice, when Doyle is in his house, must be his alone."

Link's smile came slowly into place. "Why, we wouldn't have it any other way."

CHAPTER 3

The most remarkable thing has just happened!

I have found myself standing—great Lord, how grand to be erect again, no longer entirely helpless—just inside the front door of my house! There was no sensation of movement; I did not hear anyone come to fetch me; I have no recollection of coming here!

But here I am, thank God, in *my own house!* Whatever's happened, that surely means I am both alive, and well!

"Louise?"

There was no reply, no rustling sound to indicate she was putting down whatever she was doing and hurrying to embrace me. It is a strange feeling to have no idea how long I have been away, whether it is days or weeks. All I know for sure, other than how marvelous it is to be home, is that I want to take my lovely woman into my arms, caress her sandy-blonde hair, feel her soft body willingly pressed against mine, and kiss her until nothing else matters. *Welcome back, tiger!*

Suddenly I felt a little dizzy as a thought occurred to me, and I braced myself against the wall. What, I wondered, if I am hallucinating? Somewhere I read, years ago, that a man could only be in total isolation for so long a period of time before his mind cracked down the middle. Perhaps mine was going, or gone. Because I had not only been alone but in absolute darkness, without a sight or sound of any distinguishable kind. For a . . . long time?

Crazy, but I put my hand over my eyes just for a moment then; blackness had temporarily become my home and when I renewed it by blocking out my own comfortable living room, it was a steadying factor. I remembered seeing an old Lee Marvin program on television when I was a kid, I think it was a true story, and Lee was in captivity—probably in Korea—and isolation. There came a time when he knew, unless he did something, he would go absolutely mad and he'd already counted every brick in the wall and mentally written a thousand letters home. So you know what he did? He stared at that impenetrable wall and began, piece by piece, assembling pictures on it. He saw his Mom, he saw his Dad, he saw his wife and little girl one after another, *willing* them to come to the wall like slow-motion electronic impulses on a television set. And . . .

What the hell am I talking about! What did that old flick have to do with anything?

I shoved myself off the wall and ventured into the dining room, then the kitchen. Outside in back, I knew, was the garage with my loft—my den or study—above it. And a book I was working on when *it* happened is just waiting for the author to finish it. For the second time I managed a smile. En route to the kitchen I saw the way Louise had left a half-completed jigsaw puzzle on the card table—*piece by piece; electronic impulses*—and a book left open with an ashtray set on top of it. The phone wasn't plugged in, which seemed silly, since there was no one home to object to it. How like Louise; how I *liked* Louise, wanted to see her.

There, in the kitchen, my dog Angelo was pressed against the cabinets beneath the sink, cowering. Whining. A St. Bernard, he was so huge that he looked almost as ridiculous as he looked pathetic—and bewildering.

Why hadn't the old boy come galloping out to throw his big paws on my chest and lap my face with his rough tongue?

I was within three feet of him, reaching out to rub his soft head and assure him that everything was fine, when I heard the panting begin. It was a terrible sound, a warning. Not a warning that he was going to bite me—Angelo bit nothing but a random flea—but a warning that he might by God have a *heart attack* if I touched him! *He was scared to death of me!*

I tried a lot of "It's all right, boy"s and "Come here, fella"s and "Don't you know me, Angelo"s but it was worse than no effort at all. His eyes had rolled 'way back in his head with the whites showing as if he was soon to meet his Maker and might be making some kind of mumbling, soft-hearted canine prayer for deliverance.

Sick, I told myself. Angelo is sick. I checked his food bowl and water dish. Not surprisingly, the former was almost empty but not enough for him to starve. The big pig ate until he was stuffed. He had ample water. Eddie, Louise's kid, was forever ransacking the freezer for ice cubes on the theory that if Angelo was actually a member of the family, he was entitled to a decent drink too. One quarter of a cube remained in the bowl now. So that meant *somebody* had been here in the last hour or so.

The door to the basement was ajar. Only half a foot or so; ajar. It was dark as hell down there and I thought about going down to see if somebody was there, if someone hadn't heard me because he was working in the utility room.

Except something extraordinary happened to me when I slipped into the aperture and began fumbling for the light: *I broke out in a cold sweat, the hair on the back of my neck seemed to stand on end, and I knew that something was telling me not to go down there.* Something or *somebody*. But the crazy thing was afterward and it hit me hard. *I was becoming sexually aroused.* I have no idea why, since Louise and I have confined our activities to the bedroom right from the start—Eddie was there, even before Tommy—but the impact was powerful. It was kind of like when I was in my teens and found a cache of my dad's old back issues of *Playboy*, where I wasn't supposed to be, and sat there for an hour looking at wonders I'd only suspected. The impact had been so great that I didn't touch myself, didn't even realize I was aroused; because every damn one of those incredible pictures had to be savored, one by one; and the heat inside me kept on rising until I was dizzy.

My own basement did a thing like that to me? I backed off from the door, staring at it like an idiot. I thought of *pheremones*, the odor animals in heat give off, how it's almost something tangible to the male of the species, and wondered if Louise had been visited by the next Sex Goddess of Hollywood. Really, there was no clear explanation for it and again I put out my hand, reaching into the space between the door and wall for the light switch, before I remembered the first feeling that had hit me. It was some kind of—of cosmic *warning*, I thought; wasn't there some kind of old Quincy-like rumor that men died with an erection? Had my guardian angel put in a belated appearance and warned me that, if I went downstairs, the Last One was going to be a daisy?

Angelo was no longer leaning helplessly against the cabinets. He'd taken off for dear life, scared shitless of the guy who picked him out of the whole damned litter and brought him home to Eddie and Tommy stuck under his coat like the worst kept secret in the world. Pregnant with immense puppy, father and child doing well. I have to admit that I felt terribly resentful; immaturely without a doubt, but hurt. The way it had turned out, Angelo was my dog all the way. *I* was the one he looked forward to seeing, even if Louise did feed him most of the time; and now the miserable cur had spooked.

What if I am dead?

The notion crept on snail feet back into my mind without an instant's warning. In a way, it was just suddenly there, and I couldn't stop it. I told myself that I hadn't actually *thought* it at all, that it was placed in my brain like the warning not to go down to the basement, but it didn't do much good. All I knew, when I began to rationalize it, was what an assy idea it was. Wasn't I in my own house at last, standing up like a man and messing around, puttering, the way I'd done a million times before?

Electronic impulses. Piece by piece.

I went upstairs to look for somebody, anybody. The neighbor's goddamn *cat* could have gotten in and peed on the bed, the way he did last spring, if he'd only have the decency to recognize me and let me throw him out. Or, the way I felt then, pet him.

I noticed for the first time how the carpeting was getting thin on—let's see—the fourth and ninth steps up, and made a mental note to do something about it. Then it occurred to me, with a start, how dusty everything looked in the house. Like it was even more neglected than usual—I'm no handyman and Louise hates housework. Except then, as I stepped into the bathroom and saw how much we needed new tiling, it occurred to me that the house wasn't really so much dusty or neglected as it was . . . *older*.

Oh, for Christ's sake, how long had I been in that crappy . . . hospital?

My bedroom. *Our* bedroom. A lovely place. Not to anybody else who stepped in there, I suppose, but lovely to me. Just as much a retreat as my study over the garage but in a different way, a *shared* way. I was surprised to see that Louise had actually made the bed before nightfall, and sat down on the edge of the mattress for a minute, fiddling with the blanket. I sighed, loudly. Nobody knew how much he loved his home until he was away from it for awhile in the hospital. No one knew how it felt sort of *sacred*, almost; I supposed that was what they used to mean by the sanctity of the home and family.

My closet door was open. Unlike the door to the basement, wide open. I stayed right there on the bed, staring into it with unbelieving eyes. I couldn't even begin to figure out what had happened, *why* it was like that, and for a long while my mind wouldn't even accept it.

My closet was empty. My two suits, my four pair of slacks, my God-knows-how-many shirts in God-knew what state of repair, those neckties I'd always hated to wear, even the unsightly wide ones from circa 1969— *gone.* Hauled off somewhere; removed, stolen, heisted and lifted. The closet was empty right down to where my shoes used to be on the shoerack and an old painting my mom left me when she died. Zilch.

Louise stood in the doorway of the bedroom, frozen.

Human nature has to be the weirdest thing in the world. I'd thought largely of her, while I was away; if I'd counted the thoughts, Louise was the clear winner by a mile. When I got back to the house I'd called *her* name first.

So being a human being I looked up at her now, and snapped: "Where the hell have you taken my clothes to? What'd you *do* with them?"

There was no reply and I knew I'd blown it, right off the bat, spoiled the reunion for both of us. She came into the bedroom, shaking her head a little as if she'd felt a draft or heard some vagrant sound at a distance, and began undressing.

I'll admit I was shocked. Under the ceiling light—something I'd insisted upon when we moved here; I wanted to *see* my woman without clothes, not conjure up an old *Playboy* image from a creepy bedlamp—Louise had aged a great deal. Why, there was actually gray in the waves of her hair now, and the skin beneath her pretty eyes and in her cheeks was sagging a little.

My heart went out to her. I don't know that I ever loved her more than I did right that second. Obviously, she'd been worried sick about me. And just as obviously, that meant I'd been away for more than merely days.

Amnesia! The word vaulted to my mind. "I've had *amnesia!* Because *I've been gone a year or more!*"

When she removed her blouse and began unzipping her skirt, I got up from the bed to cross the room toward her. I was ready to apologize the entire night, if that was what it took. Anything to hold Louise in my arms close, closer. I was filled with a deep, painful yearning, a giving kind of love that was different in uncanny ways than any I'd ever felt for anyone. A love which contained elements of fresh wisdom, I think, a kind new to me; fragments of wan wistfulness, yes, and a searing regret that I'd never been a better man. She'd deserved the best.

Smiling, I put my arms around her.

"God," she said softly, flinching away, "it's *cold* in here . . ."

Her comment did not immediately register, however. I was watching the way my arms, as I reached for her, *passed directly through the suntanned skin of her bare back and the well-filled white bra, and seemed to enfold nothing but my own, wanting body.*

I blinked like a lunatic as her words got through, as Louise shuddered and moved away. I hadn't touched her at all. I couldn't.

I could not touch my own wife!

I shrieked then. It was a lot more than screaming, it had terror and supplication in it. I shrieked right into that face I loved, even as I shot my arms behind my back and hoped I'd never seem them or my hands again. I shrieked; then I shrieked again.

But she didn't hear.

"I wish you were with me, Zach," she said. There was immense longing in her voice and I knew at once, that it was not really addressed to me—not to the "me" I'd been. Yet maybe my shouting had produced some strange kind of energy, and it bestirred the soundwaves of our bedroom, *reminded* her of me. "We really should get the storm windows up."

Louise bit her lip, then slipped quickly out of her skirt and put on a robe. The robe was very pretty, a gift to her from me at Christmas-time.

At Christmas-Past, I thought, shaking the chains of my memory and staring at her as she walked through the door, leaving me alone in the bedroom.

A mistake. I said that aloud. *Some awful mistake*

35

has been made. There's no way it's the way it looks. I knew then that if being haunted was frightening, *haunting* was a much worse thing.

Yet, sweet heaven, the question was certainly inescapable: *what if I am dead now?*

CHAPTER 4

During most of the period of time it took for Newton Link to get authorization for the man, Zachary Edson Doyle, to make his own choice of hereafters, the plump, white-suited Chauncey Wells cooled his heels in the corporate lounge. Except that cooling much of anything was a problem down here. "We exist in a universe of cliches," he mumbled, sipping strong coffee that he didn't really want.

The temperature of the entire structure appeared to be maintained at an undeviating eight-five degrees, and all the employees he encounterred looked perfectly comfortable. Because of the effort each agent made to remain up-to-date, Wells was aware of the role that consistent symbolism played in the success of the modern firm on, above, or below earth. Still and all, finding nothing but hot drinks and indigestible food that had to be cooked in miniature microwave ovens seemed a bit much. He seriously doubted that any visitors to Link's corporation would be scandalized (or corrupted) by a few bottles of Pepsi Cola or Nehi, or a machine that dispensed iced tea. As nearly as Wells could detect, there wasn't even a water cooler anywhere to quench his thirst. There were six coffee machines, and cocoa, soups of every variety, but nothing that would provide a heavyset man with the heavenly cool drink for which he'd begun to thirst.

Sometimes he thought hell was distinguishable more for its stubbornness and bad taste than its sin.

In the lounge he pored through certain Washington, New York and Cuban newspapers several times, including a complete back file of the Russian *Pravda* and some one-sheet newsletter in an Oriental language, and then gave up in disgust. He went in search of the company library, looking for something readable.

On the thirty-second floor he found himself stopped in front of a dead-end, locked and bolted iron door with PRIVATE—NO EXCEPTIONS stamped in letters of flaming red. There was even an electric eye setup in clear view to deter any unwelcome visitors who might jiggle the handle. Wells paused momentarily and shuddered. The heat from behind the door was stifling, unbearable; it crept out beneath the door like palpable fingers reaching to drag him in. Wells growled a prayer that was nearly an imprecation and continued looking for the library.

Finally locating it, he was instantly appalled by the collection. While it was true that he seriously disapproved of the majority of books he found on the shelves, he was more dismayed by the obvious censorship that had been applied. While there were histories about famous generals, a few about inventors and a great many about well-known political figures all over the world, there were no volumes at all by or about people without sordid reputations. And the fiction— Great Scott!—should have been printed in asbestos. He was flipping irritably through a book by Aleister Crowley when a young page found him.

"Mr. Link has word for you now," the Oriental lad informed him. "He'd like you to go to his office, immediately, yes?"

"Thank God," Wells muttered, ignoring the shocked expression on the youth's face. "Another hour in this place and I'd be obliged to suffer extra church attendance for the next decade!"

Link greeted him at the door to his sumptuous office, gesturing imperatively to beckon Chauncey inside. "Come in, come in, please. I have everything neatly solved."

"Good fellow," the fat agent murmured approvingly.

"Don't you know any other adjectives but that?" the dapper man demanded. Then he shrugged, indicating his chair. "Do take a seat and hear my good news. I'm happy to report that downstairs is willing to go along with the Doyle haunting. As a matter of fact, Wells, Doyle is already in his house."

Chauncey's wide nostrils quivered with suspicion. "I find that a trifle presumptuous. I should have been present when he was released from his grave."

"You wanted him set loose, didn't you?" Link asked with some asperity. "Let's not carp about the arrangements at the last moment."

Chauncey Wells had settled into his chair across from his opposite number, his round jaws set. For a moment he tapped his fingertips thoughtfully on the arm of his chair. Finally he waved a well-padded hand at the viewing screen in the corner. "I want to see the video tape of what has happened to date. I must be informed; my people expect it."

"I fail to see the point of that," Link argued, tugging neatly at his trouser knees before slowly sitting. "It's quite routine, don't you agree? Your Mr. Doyle is walking the floors of the house he used to own, unaware that living people cannot see him. Except a handful of psychics, of course, and I am reliably informed that none of his family fits that description. Once he makes a choice about his ultimate destination, the entire matter is closed."

"It is precisely that last element that concerns me," replied Wells, his expression unyielding. "Come, come, Newton—good fellow, I wasn't dead yesterday, you know." He planted his hands on his thighs to lean forward. "What little, ah, *enticements* have you managed to present for the poor man's temptation?"

"My dear Wells!"

"Do I get to see what's transpired or do I invalidate the new agreement? Frankly, whatever the changes that would be wrought and the enormous paper work, I'd just as soon the Second Coming become a reality at once."

For a moment Newton Link glared helplessly, angrily, at his obese guest. At last he made an elegant gesture, drew himself up with dignity, and pushed a button on his control panel. The doors covering the television screen slid back and a picture came quickly into focus.

Wells risked a smile. The video tape was already in place, Link obviously knowing that his demands would be made. The dapper statistician had simply attempted a bluff.

He watched as Zach Doyle opened the front door of his house and entered, heard the man call his widow's name, saw him wander out to the dining room. The jigsaw puzzle on the card table, he observed with gratification, depicted the interior of a famous cathedral in Rome. With an uprising of compassion, Wells saw what had happened when Doyle tried to pat his animal. Even on video tape, with the special Black Hole feature given the film that they used, Doyle's face and figure had a dim, verging-on-disappearing quality that, after considerable exposure to the process, Wells found vaguely disturbing. Once the man's selection was made, and whichever way he went, the transition would be completed and—to Wells and Link, at least —he would look like anybody else.

He saw Zach Doyle approach the door to his basement—*and saw the TV image begin to flicker violently*. The series of manically zigzagging lines crossing the screen made Chauncey Wells blink, and wonder if he were being exposed to the subliminal propagandizing which had begun in this section of after-death. The words appeared: WE ARE EXPERIENCING TECHNICAL DIFFICULTY. PLEASE STAND BY.

Wells, glaring at Link, was on the verge of stating the obvious: that a fiendish deception was being used to sting not only Zachary Doyle but him, Chauncey Wells. Clearly, the breakup in the picture was intentional; Link had not wanted him to see what was happening.

Before he could make his accusation, an image of Doyle mounting the stairs, was again in view. *Very well*, thought Wells, *let's play this differently*. Surely Link hadn't believed the deception would work, and pretending innocence might bring the handsome devil into the open. It would also allow time for reflection.

And Wells saw, then, what he had not been able to see on the TV screen. Either romantic or sexual enticement was being utilized by Newton Link in the basement of the Doyle home in an effort to make the poor shade symbolically *make a commitment to Hell!* It infuriated the obese angel, but he should have anticipated as much. Like and his people wouldn't allow Doyle to make the decision unaided; whatever trickery was necessary would be put into operation, despite Wells' agreement with Link.

But for now, all right. Because Chauncey Wells had made a few little seductive arrangements of his own by virtue of contacting his own headquarters from the lounge, arrangements which meant that if Zachary Edson Doyle left the house and walked into his former study over the garage it would officially be considered a symbolic choice in favor of Wells' side.

Trying to decide what was right and what was wrong had always been hard, from time to time; but now, in Chauncey Wells' view, it was harder than ever. It was true that, like Link, he had betrayed the spirit of their ongoing agreement by phoning headquarters; he might even have been a few minutes earlier with his call than Link had been with his. In Wells' early period as a representative of the forces for good, such an action might have brought him up on charges, even found him dismissed from the heavenly agency. But shiny, shimmering "sophistication," a word that had been held in high favor for several decades, was something some of his superiors approved and they understood perfectly the way Wells had read the situation: Newton Link could not be trusted; Link would definitely take covert action; ergo, Chauncey Wells was under the same obligation.

Whether his certain knowledge about the evil chap meant that Link had initiated unacceptable measures or Link would have needed to take them *before* Wells reacted—that, the heavyset angel knew, was a question of fine print for superiors in both organizations to haggle over. In any case, each side knew perfectly well that the balance of power had to be sustained; neither knew exactly what would happen if, after thousands of years, all negotiations were broken off forever.

The two agents saw Zach enter his bedroom, perch on the edge of the bed, and become incredulous as discovery followed discovery. For Wells, who'd never fully banished the essential purity of heart that had earned him his wings, it was awful waiting for Doyle's widow to arrive and even worse when she did. The shock to his psychic systems would be considerable; it might even be an eventual determinant of the choice he made. And when it actually happened and Louise Doyle did not realize Zach was pathetically holding her, Wells looked away from the screen.

By then, however, he was merely trying to figure a means not only to assuage the human spirit's sorrow but to guide him outstairs to the garage loft. The sooner it was over, the better for all concerned—especially Zachary Doyle, and except for Newton Link.

Which reminded Wells that Link looked exceptionally sanguine and relaxed, and could not be taken for granted. A wary glint shone in the angel's tiny, bishop-sharp eyes as Link responded to the gaze upon him with a relaxed smile Wells found disturbingly sinister.

Hell was never more dangerous, or ruthless, than when its representatives smiled—or when you believed that you were truly safe, or saved. This might prove to be an extremely difficult, even hazardous, competition.

CHAPTER 5

It was tough the first day when the boys came home from school. And the second day, and the third, etc. I was so glad to see them both, especially my Tommy, that I wanted to hug each of them to me and explain that their old man was back to stay.

Except I don't appear to be as much a man of substance as once I was, and I don't suppose I shall ever forget the way it was to put my arms around Louise . . . and feel nothing. A cold shiver, that's what she got out of it; an unpleasant sensation that she wasn't alone. A man does not place revulsion at the top of his list for Ways His Wife Reacts. It's the ultimate frigid woman making a guy feel castrated but carried several degrees on up the ladder of shame.

And except that my boys aren't really little at all anymore, and seem to have made a fine adjustment.

Eddie, Louise's son, is seventeen while Tommy is twelve, pushing thirteen hard. During dinner, I sort of hovered around on the fringes and finally, gingerly, took the extra seat at the table, the one that used to be mine. I kept quiet and, after awhile, learned that absolute alienation can be pleasant enough if you don't take it too seriously. At least I got caught up on what Eddie and Tom were doing at school, what was on their minds (or at least what they were willing to talk about to their mother), and enjoyed hearing Louise speak normally.

As I indicated, that was a distant sort of fun for awhile. Eventually, though, I got agitated all over again and couldn't figure out exactly why I felt that way. Since they were paying no damn attention to me, I tuned them out for awhile—Louise was bringing in a Boston cream pie from Roslyn's for dessert; my favorite—and tried to understand my annoyance.

The realization of why I was troubled intensified the emotion itself. For several longish moments I gaped at them, my hands on the dining table bracing me—although I guess I could have fallen right into the remainder of homemade vegetable soup without even making a splash—because I was so shocked by what I came to realize:

They were going on, in a very normal way, *without me.*

Sure; I know. Every time we face an insurance general agent and hear the old speech pouring out of his benignly alarming lips we get a hint of the truth, that dismal, frigid truth that the world surely goes on without us. And we shiver some, no more than when we read a horror novel or see a spooky movie; and our unconscious minds accept that drivel sent down by the conscious intelligence, stir it around awhile, and report back stoutly that it is simply Untrue. Intellectually indigestible. Why (expostulates our vainglorious ids) the whole frigging *world* will mourn us when we go. TV programs will be interrupted by sadness-instigating news breaks: GARY CLAPSADDLE DIED AT 66: ALMA PIERSON EXPIRED TODAY IN HER HOME AT LOWER BOONDOGGLE: WE INTERRUPT REGULAR PROGRAMMING WITH THE SAD NEWS THAT JOHN P. SMITH, WELL-KNOWN OFFICE MANAGER AND AMATEUR CARPENTER, HAS SUCCUMBED. Soon people are on their phones to everyone they know, using the kind of terms they used when John F. Kennedy was shot in Dallas; afterward, in the same manner, everybody will always know Where They Were and What They Were Doing the day that Betty or Claude Got Theirs.

But the conscious, logical mind was right after all. I saw that now with the utmost clarity. Louise Callahan Doyle and sons were going on with life, not the "best way they could" but as if one Zachary Edon Doyle had never existed. Look, folks, no sweat: Pop's gone. It would almost be better if they were cheering.

And so I confronted the embarrassing and lugubrious *secondary* fact that, when we say courageously to our loved ones, "I hope you'll adjust easily when I'm no longer around," we are lying in our goddamn *teeth!* That's only what we boast when we have a key birthday—like 30, 40, or 50—and feel great, like worldbeaters who'll always be there, who have all the time in the world.

It's bullshit that we want you to adjust, easily or otherwise, I realized wryly and, as I noted, with the good graces of embarrassment. We want you to *remember us forever*, at least as often as if we were just at work or playing golf or working in the kitchen or jogging. More! We hope that every decent thing we ever did will remain deepdown *appreciated;* we want you to find tears in your eyes every time you mention our name, which, by rights, should be in every third sentence. We want you to *grieve like hell* when we're "gone," to find that your life will *never* be "The way it was" again. We certainly don't want you to sit there at the supper table burping your soup and salad, and stuffing your lousy living faces with Boston cream pie!

So it turns out to be a mental tie: logical conscious, 1; self-sentimental and egotistical unconscious, 1. There will be no sudden-death overtime.

Unless what I have now, God help me, is It.

That first awful night I was back I watched television with my little family the way I'd done so casually and ungratefully a million times, unaware of what I had going for me, and every now and then went over to the *TV Guide* lying on a table by Louise's elbow, picked out a good cops-and-robbers show, or a drama with a little meat, and loudly complained about what Louise had checked. Right off they switched on some goddamn sitcom, or later stared at a documentary on some vital topic like Hair Styling Secrets of the Stars, the CIA in Laos, or The Private Partygoing World of

John Travolta. Occasionally, when I was clearing my throat or sounding off, I'd sit on the edge of Tommy's chair and ruffle his blond hair, which stayed adamantly in place, or ask Louise to fix me a nice glass of iced tea. By the end of the evening, fed up with feeling ignored, I was getting a little snotty: "What about a highball, Lou, or some expensive wine? Since the Head of the House returned home, at last, why not pheasant under glass for a midnight snack? Louise, *you listening?*"

She wasn't, although I began realizing that I was bothering her a little. And that wasn't the goal. I might want her to remember me, but I didn't actually want to be the one who caused her discomfort. In any case, my nerves were in a marvelous state by the time we went to bed.

Yes, I said "we." I watched her undress and learned that the sensual vibes issuing from our basement weren't the only thing that still made me hot. I suppose, if there'd been a woman who realized I was around, I might have been happy to learn that there *was* Sex After Death. But Louise paraded around naked, taking a bath and putting her hair up, and my newfound post-life arousal became just one more hardship to bear.

I think I can imagine how you feel about all this. I can see you shudder, like I was a succubus or some goddamn monster. The image of a dead man—a ghost, a *ghoul*, from your standpoint—lying beside his living, bareass wife makes you a little sick at your stomach. Well, I'm sorry. They only made it "until death do you part" because they lacked the faith in their own doctrine of Paradise to realize that someone might still be around, wanting a little. Or a little affection.

The first time I cupped my hand around her round, brown-tipped breast, she flicked at it as if a fly had landed on it. When she flipped over on her tummy to read—hell, I saw it wasn't even one of my books!—I put my lips on her sweetly-remembered cheek and kissed her. For a moment she ignored it; there was no reaction. When I tried it again, however, she reached down to pull the covers up over her back and shoulders.

Talk about blazing sex appeal! Man, I am *loaded* with charm! One touch from my flaming lips and every woman turns up the thermostat!

The only advantage I could detect just then was that I could walk around Monument Circle in downtown Indianapolis stark naked, thumbing my nose at the police and making unfelt bodily passes at the lasses, and no one would notice. Dirty old man in a raincoat of death. Even though I have never been much of a voyeur or exhibitionist, I filed the thought away for future reference.

If nobody's going to come collect me, I have to find *some* way to get my jollies.

The tone of braggadocio in these mental notes I have begun is making me start to gag; but if I stop trying to find the light side of nothingness, I am truly lost.

At last Louise turned off the light and I arose just as she began to snore. No problem in disturbing her these days if I had to go to the bathroom at night. The mattress didn't so much as budge when my weight shifted, mainly because I do not seem to have any. Death, I have learned, is an instant weight loss program that really works! As a writer, maybe that best seller I've sought so long will turn out to be the new hit diet book, *The Wraith's Way to Weight Reduction* (or *Be Thin as a Wraith*). Maybe *You're One Minute Away from a Perfect Figure*. Or even, more suggestively and more horrendously, *Your Do-It-Yourself Death Diet*.

I must become more amusing to myself or find the laughs turn to tears.

Thinking of writing gave me the idea of writing—typing—a message to Louise, some indication that I am still, in a loose manner of speaking, alive although I've died. You see, I had no clear idea of what I could and could not do, just as an infant does not automatically know he can walk, win grades, kiss girls, or grow up to be president. When I mentioned going to the bathroom during the night I really had no idea whether there was a need for such gross human actions anymore. I had suffered no hunger, for example, even when Louise toted out the Boston cream pie to the who-cares-about-Pop? cheers of my son.

Whether I had the—*power? energy? ectoplasm?*—necessary to press my fingertips on typewriter keys and make the first impression I'd made since I got back (ha-ha; another bad joke) I did not know.

But suddenly, as I stood in my street clothes by the bed that used to be partly mine, I had to find out. I blew a kiss to the restlessly sleeping Louise and reached for my bathrobe, not even surprised for a minute that it was still in the house. She'd always liked it and now it seemed she'd kept it for herself. But the old Indian Giver needed it now; it was winter, and my topcoat had long since been given to Goodwill. Or perhaps my brother Harry, whom I haven't spoken to in eight years this February. The trouble was, when I tried to pick it up, the robe, a joint gift from Eddie and Tommy, doubtlessly selected and paid for by Louise, since my kids never had time or money for affection, my hands passed right through it.

That threw me for a loop, almost back into black depression. What saved me was sheer curiosity. Looking down at myself, I saw that I still wore my best three-piece deep blue suit and impulsively-purchased Gucci loafers—or, at any rate, *seemed* to wear them. When I touched my other sleeve, the material was there and felt perfectly natural. That, I thought, opened up a can of exceptional questions; for example, that nudity appeared to be repudiated and outlawed by the Geneva Convention of Keepers of the Just Dead. Like a prison warden waving a fond farewell to a paroled life convict, they gave you your suit and whatever spare change you might find tucked in the lining. (Would a modern version of the Egyptian pharaoh surrounded by food and treasures inn his eerie pyramid be a clean-shaven dead American in a suit from Sears with a Master Charge card in his breast pocket?) Or perhaps it was more complex than that and psychometrists, who claimed they could trace the identity or location of a person from the mere touch of his possessions, were right after all. That the things you took with you into the casket, in effect, went right with you on the trip but that every other thing you might care to touch or caress no longer shared the same reality? If so, shocking as it was to consider, some of the oddball religious cults who killed your wife and mistresses in order to leave them lying next to you might have something there. Wouldn't the ERA ladies have a fit at such a suggestion?

For a minute I stood there, looking like an idiot, feeling first my handmade shirt and then trying but *not* feeling a final bottle of my old aftershave on the dresser; *not* feeling one of Louise's fuzzy red bedroom slippers and then reaching into my hip pocket—it occurred to me that everything about me had a funny smell, these days—and both feeling and tugging out a brand new six-dollar silk handkerchief. I peered at it in the gloom of the midnight bedroom, feeling quizzical as hell.

Louise and the mortician had arranged to bail me out in case my nose ran after I was dead, dressed me fit to kill, but hadn't given me my typewriter, a change of clothes, my favorite brand of musk aftershave, or even a damned charge card. What one wanted to make of that peculiar selection process I had no idea, but I wondered if I'd died and been buried nude, if I'd be obliged to spend eternity as Zach the Flasher.

Suddenly there was so much to write down it seemed very important to learn if I could still use a typewriter or if they—whoever and whatever *they* might be—had taken that ability from me too. I went jogging off downstairs, foolishly on tiptoe. I saw that my lovable dog Angelo didn't even budge or whimper when I passed him and sought to open the front door.

My hands went right through the doorknob. Without hesitation, without the anger and fear I would earlier have felt, I took two steps backward and then *hurled* myself at the locked door.

Unnecessary waste of energy. Or ectoplasm. I passed through the door like a hot knife through butter —I can think of happier, more vulgar similes—and landed, asprawl, in snow that was gathering on the foot stoop. There was no pain which, I thought, might mean that there was something to say for death, and my good suit hadn't been torn. As a matter of fact, I noticed it wasn't even wet from the damp snow.

I clambered easily, rather lightly onto my Gucci-clad feet and blinked out at the streetlamp across the way. For a long while I stood there, pretending that I really *felt* the brisk winter air nipping my cheeks, drawing cleanly into my lungs; and I thought of Ernie Kazankus and his wife Emily in bed next door; and when I couldn't pretend any longer. I suddenly became very sad. It occurred to me that this was all a big gyp, apparently pointless; worse, it became clear to me that if I could not get the people who loved me even to notice I was there, I had very little reason to remain. (Naked on the Circle, I remembered; all the grabass any gross Italian could crave.) (Postscript notion that disgusted me: I could wander anywhere I wanted and see all the beautiful, naked women a man ever desired.) But I'd never been a promiscuous man; I was always uncomfortable around females who even seemed to come on to me. For the first time it occurred to me that maybe, when I got up in the den-loft over my garage—which I yearned to do with a new feeling that it was absolutely *imperative*—I would simply write four little words on my Royal: "I'll always love you."

Then it was off for—where? Why, anywhere I wanted to go! If you could learn to do completely without people, it mightn't be all bad. A ghost was free to step onto any jet he wished and go anywhere in the world without it costing him a penny. I found a little enthusiasm moving inside me, and worked on it, like a child works on a scab, aggravating it. Hell, I could see everywhere I had ever craved to go, and I had all the time in the world!

Abruptly the den-loft sounded like paradise and I took three excited, quick steps forward—*only to run headlong into an invisible barrier*.

Apparently it began a few inches, squareshaped, around my location when I had returned to my home. I pressed my fingertips up and down, then side to side, in all directions, but I couldn't get through it. The shield was absolute, impregnable. It would not, I thought numbly, hurt by the insight, be there for anyone else. Eddie trying to pass through might perhaps feel a chill, a vagrant throbbing breeze. Louise might go back inside for a scarf. But this was *my* reality, another thoughtful little gift from some unseen and mute guide of my destiny—and I almost thought I heard him laugh, then, at my frustration—and I hated that cosmic sucker just then more than I'd ever hated anyone in my life.

I did the only thing I had left to do.

I went back upstairs to lie beside my wife, weeping softly, and waiting for Real People to awaken in the morning and let the Perpetual Spectator watch jealously what Life was all about.

Only as I drifted off to a relatively merciful sleep I wished ardently that I had the chance, one more day, to live life *fully*, knowing it could be snatched away at any moment and remembering, as the poet had it, to smell the roses.

CHAPTER 6

The next morning, bright and early, I was sleeping soundly—*gone* is more like it, for what I do now at times of relaxation—when Louise awakened and swung her long, slender legs over the edge of the bed. Sunlight spilled in my eyes, not as sharply as before but enough to be disturbing, and just for an instant, I frowned at my wife and said something archly critical.

She had no idea I'd spoken, of course. Her/my bathrobe-clad back was to me, slumped in last-second stupor, and when I realized that she was still completely unaware of my presence, I muttered my complaints into my pillow. It was plumped, still. If I weighed anything, it wasn't enough to disturb something as soft as a pillow.

It really didn't seem fair to me that the rules claimed living people should never be disturbed by the dead but it was okay for ghosts to be exploded into consciousness by those still of the earth. She went to shower and I avoided assiduously looking at her nakedness, nearly terrified now of being aroused by it. That was when I saw with some surprise that I was still wearing my suit, and that it was as unrumpled as if I'd taken it down from a hangar. That gave me some inkling into the question of why 17th Century ghosts were still running around haunting English towers in clothing styles of their age.

Lord, I mused, finally sitting up and stretching, *I hope I don't sweat when I get myself collected at last. If there's no change of clothes, I'll smell like the Indiana Pacer gym after no more than a couple of hundred years!*

Until Louise finished her shower, I contented myself by trying to figure out the clothing thing. Underwear, socks, shoes, trousers, shirts and jackets were all things of this world, so what business did they have going along into a life beyond the grave?

The fallacy of my question came to mind seconds later, however inadequate it is: I, too, had been a "thing of this world." But *I* was there, and *I* could not be seen by the living.

When she came back into the bedroom in her panties, her gorgeous breasts swinging free, I looked away with another pang. Then, occasionally glancing her direction with little movements of my head, like a pervert beneath the stands at Hickle Fieldhouse, I waited for her. Waited like an overgrown, very pale—pale, hell, translucent!—boy for my wife to choose our activity of the day. She dressed herself in a pair of old jeans which neatly displayed her round fanny and—another twinge of agony here, yet strangely a treat, in a way—an old white short-sleeved shirt of mine. I found myself wanting to protest that it was still a good shirt and wasn't ready to be used for physical work.

Yet I didn't attempt to stop her. I'd seen how grand it was to realize that *something* of me, or mine, was close to her breathing, warm flesh again.

I trailed downstairs after her and listened to breakfast conversation between Louise and her boy, Eddie. For awhile, it was pleasant enough. I pretended to be reading the morning paper or maybe working on the outline for a new book, instead of dead. But then, some odd things happened.

I realized, to start with, that Eddie was lying through his teeth.

The thing is, I've never been very good at spotting kids' falsehoods. Louise, to be honest about it, was always the shrewd, disbelieving parent. I'd worked fairly hard at letting her be the hard-hat which of course permitted me to look like the good guy.

Now it wasn't anything especially obvious Eddie said. Somehow, though, I *knew* deep inside that Eddie intended to buy coke that afternoon, and not the kind that comes in ice-cold bottles. His intention was to spend most of the evening sniffing the shit with some nogoodnik named Allen (or Alan; or Allan; I couldn't tell spellings, just internal sound-impressions).

Now, I don't want to give the impression that I was a truly unforgettable father, the kind who changes the kid's diapers, teaches him to walk, and romps with him through the fundamentals of baseball. I'm not sure I *know* the fundamentals of baseball.

And judging by what happened next, I suppose I don't even know the fundamentals of anything. Because Eddie, looking around with the guiltiest expression I ever saw, aside from the reflection in my own mirror, suddenly booked. I believe that's what some language-hating kids say these days. I mean that he cut out, left, departed; and Louise was no more than wiser.

Before he was gone, however, it came to me like a flash that I'd *read the mind* of Louise's son—and that was another big flash. Or surprise, since I've never had the slightest sign of Psi, or ESP, or any of that jazz.

Hadn't had, that is. Past tense.

Since I knew little more than the next guy about the nature of telepathy, I believed at that time, wafting around in my widow's kitchen, that it was bound to be a two-way street. Which is why I tried to zap young Eddie with the sharp objections leaping to my mind. I'm no prude, but I think nose-candy isn't dandy and a sharp blade is quicker (to mix up an old verse). I also didn't like the way the kid meant to deceive his mother, *my* wife. Or widow.

But I tried like hell and nothing happened. Eddie didn't even look like he'd felt a cold spot at the breakfast table. And when I caught an unintentional glimpse of what my own son, Tom, had in his mind and he, too, did not respond to my anxious mental projections, well, it was a real downer.

Tom was going to buy some cocaine from his halfbrother.

Whether I should be ashamed to say so or not, I discovered tears in my eyes—invisible ones, I supposed; nobody gave a damn, anyway—and simply sat there as both boys left the house, ready to meet the man, the pusher, the lousy sleaze who fattened his own billfold or his own doped-up head at the expense of children.

I was so dismayed, I remembered the first feelings I'd had when I started to go downstairs to the basement, arose, and had walked noiselessly across the kitchen floor.

There'd been a battery of sensations rising up those rickety steps and strumming my psychic, sensual nerves like old Les Paul trying out a new guitar. I'd longed to descend; it was as if the rich perfume at the throat of a lovely woman had made a pledge that I'd get to see and taste and smell the rest of her and would not be disappointed.

At the door, though, I remembered the second impression—warning signals of danger, just as palpable and not nearly as much fun to consider. Impressions of soul-searing hazard, despair, perpetual ugliness and psychic blight all mine for the asking, just be opening the door to my own basement.

I wondered that second—although the idea appeared in my mind as if propelled from outside, and not any brain-activity upon my own part—what earthly thing could hurt me now, anyway; but as the encouraging concept took form, my mind also accepted the seemingly-projected though, "Who said it was *earthly*?"

And Louise arose to answer a knock at the front door.

I went along with her, totally without any appreciation for my manners on *her* part, of course, and gazed with surprise after she'd opened the door.

Three blacks stood there, polite and patient enough, and they had the look of people who'd been invited. I realized quickly that I was looking at three generations of the same family: a boy whose willingness to work with his elders clearly compromised all the child labor laws, but whose grin told me he didn't mind. A handsome man in his mid-thirties, who looked like a combination of the Doctor, Julius Erving, and sleek Roger Brown of the old Pacer basketball team. And an aged, smiling man with grizzled white hair and a distinct stoop. What did they want?

Louise wasn't surprised at all. "Oh, good!" she exclaimed. "You're here on time—even early."

Early for what? Curious, and somewhat protective of her interests (bigotry is frequently surprising to white people, especially their own and the way it happens just when you're convinced you killed all the old craziness) I hung close by. Louise's forearm passed directly through my midsection as she spun to enter the hall closet and rummage around inside. She emerged with a topcoat I'd given her for Christmas at least nine or ten years ago, and hurried out the front door with the trio at her heels. Forgetting there had been a shield or forcefield around the house to prevent me from exiting, I walked right after them, free of the house.

Whereupon more abstruse questions leaped to mind as I followed the foursome. Was I being *allowed* to expand my range of freedom? If so, didn't that mean that someone was doing the allowing—someone, or something, *somewhere?* Tagging along, I knew I would have to sit down soon, calmly, and begin trying to figure out the rationale of my circumstances, in the hope that I could learn the ground rules and make progress toward some improvement of my lot.

The grass was getting long and weeds were racing to compete along the edges of our driveway. My more-or-less idle glance raised toward the garage itself . . .

And I stopped, staring at a pickup truck. It belonged to the three visitors, I realized; it was of such ancient vintage that it was a miracle the thing would go forward without a push. From a locomotive. When I glanced at Louise, she was looking up in the direction of my creative hidey-hole.

All three of our visitors were inside the garage and the fellow closest to my age took a key from Louise, then turned to a door leading to interior steps. For the first time I realized with dismay what my wife intended for them to do.

She was getting things cleaned out of my study, my den! She was completing the widow's necessary transition, once and for all by throwing away my things!

That instant, let me tell you, I couldn't have moved and I couldn't have been moved. Gaping, shaking, I was colder than I'd have been in the flesh relentlessly clutched by Hoosier winter. My clothing was one thing; one could always replace a shirt, a suit, a pair of blue jeans—or at least, one could if he were living. These were my *personal effects* (I confess that term, the kind of person never uses about himself while he is still living, shocked me badly, miserably) and Louise was throwing away all the objects that were dearest to my heart.

Obviously she was selling them, making whatever she could to swell the widow's coffers. Such an attitude, of course, was cold, unreasonable, on my part; I understood that. Money, in life, is really the thing everyone pursues, not love or liberty, friendship, advancement of one's ideals and principles, renown or even power. Everyone except, perhaps, a handful of dumb "creative types" like me who know they call it currency because it only has a current value and who prefer to go in for more permanent gods.

Then I felt even more blue and despairing when I got it through my head that a great percentage of the Zachary Doyle "personal effects" the trio was lugging down the stairs from my study had no—what was that sinisterly-smiling term?—intrinsic value. Junkmen and a dead writer, two different interpretations of the word "priceless." Because where most of my stuff was concerned, Louise wasn't going to make out like an old-fashioned "resurrection man" at all.

She was probably paying them to haul my priceless crap away.

I'll tell you, if I'd had the faintest notion then how to haunt anybody, I'd have really scared the shit out of those guys!

Until that thought, I'd been unconsciously edging toward the foot of the stairs leading to my loft. (I thought about it under a hundred different terms, but what they all boiled down to was this: *my place.*) Maybe that unreasoning, impulsive part of my mind that acts as an idea-cellar had meant to throw myself over the valuables, or in front of the guy my age.

But then my conscious mind had apparently informed the dumb subset that if Louise could pass right through my body, so could the others. The only important thing to come out of that dreary time when I had the impression my psyche or maybe my soul was being raped was a realization that, since I *had* no physical brain left, the believing scientists who'd insisted that man had a mind apart from and overseeing the "little grey cells" of Christie's Poirot were right. And I remembered that some other bright people had replied to that assertion, "If that's so, isn't what you're talking about really that marvelous *soul* religious people used to believe in?"

Anyway, the trashmen had made several trips, toting away bookcases, a couch I'd once rescued from my wife when we bought the only new furniture of our married life, my desk chair, and several cartons of books Louise didn't seem to want. That sight sickened me, almost forced me to try a fast haunting. Surely my pet, much-thumbed thesaurus was in one of the cartons along with the valueless paperbacks of Fitzgerald, Salinger, and others—valueless except, I knew, to me.

The little boy's small arms were loaded with stacks of ashtrays, old lighters, pencils and pens. Next came the man my age. It wasn't so much what he was carrying as a sudden, childishly impetuous rage that came over me and made me wait until the guy was two steps from the garage floor.

Then I tripped him.

Or to be exact, watched my foot pass straight

through his ankle as he continued ambling down the drive, whistling in a careless, offkey manner some rhythm-and-blues ode to promiscuity and pandering.

I stood there atremble with fury and indignation. I wanted to *hurt* those people. For the first time I was turned into a sweaty, redneckcd bigot as I shook my fist after the men and virtually prayed for a way to make them as miserable as I was.

That was when I became aware of the aged black laboriously descending the steps from my hidey-hole. And I saw what he carried, in hands so dark they appeared ashen, against his aged chest.

My typewriter.

ROYAL 440, was stamped into the front of the machine. Oh, I didn't *see* it; the front was snuggled up against the old man, but I knew that typewriter better than I did my two hands. I also knew the top was gone from the contraption because I'd removed it myself a few years ago to change the ribbon quickly, and not get slowed down while the words were flowing out. Since then, I'd misplaced the top, but I didn't think the old man would mind.

Well, dammit, I minded *everything* I was seeing! This was the typewriter I'd used to establish what I was in life, the instrument that fixed my identity as an artist, a man, a provider, and promised the warm-blooded tissue of fragmentary immortality I'd foolishly believed would be enough. I'd had that surly, stiff-limbed old Royal 440 repaired every ten or twelve months for years, with minimal complaining; it was like taking one's aged father to the doctor and praying every visit that the doctor wouldn't shake his head sadly. I had cherished it for nineteen or twenty years of my life—even though, awful as it is to admit, I'd never realized that before.

And so I took a step forward, somehow hoping to stop that old gentleman; and so, finally, I noticed his *attitude*.

Attitudes are what life is about. Attitudes, when you get down to it, are more reliable than faces or expressions and all that "body language" bullcrap. If you can't be seen and you can appraise a person and really know his overall attitude about a variety of matters, well, you really know him then. And that old man's attitude was full of nice things: appreciation, happiness, dignity—and more. He carried my beat-up machine with an attitude of *respect*, the kind one rarely sees anymore.

His eyes shone with pleasure. For him, this trash pick-up wasn't just another; with me, he shared the knowledge that it was an important one. He would recall it always with delight. Why, it might have been his Find of eighty years! I watched those huge, ebon eyes glitter, I saw the way he held the typewriter with caring purposefulness, even affection; and I saw then that he was thinking about That Book. Yes; That Book, with capital letters, the one the old man had always meant to write.

I stepped out of his path then, with the kind of respect he had for my machine.

I wondered intensely, What is it you'll create, old man? In my heart, I asked him that, knowing he couldn't have heard my spoken words and not wanting to deter him any longer. But I trailed in his limping path, tears in my eyes, yearning to know. What verses do you compose in your soul, old fella? What cruel memories have refused to leave your mind and won't depart until you put them down? Is there an angry book coming, vengeance steaming along your veins, personal condemnations that storm for release? Will you decide to remind us of all those pale, petty deceits of ours which surely show a darkness of the spirit much blacker than your ebon, ashen skin? Are you moved to write, to create, in order to banish a lack of light similar to what I found when I mouldered in my grave? Will it, at last, illumine the world—and you? Enlighten us all?

I wiped away my tears as I followed him on down the driveway to my old familiar street, and I looked back at the familiar window on the second floor of our garage. Soon, I saw, it would be quite empty up there. Soon there'd be no trace remaining of Zach Doyle—or my work.

So I said, in that strange "aloud" I have come to know will not be heard, standing behind the aged man as he gravely handed the typewriter to his son seated inside the truck, "Will you write something beautiful on my Royal old pal, sir? Something . . . *beneficial? Will* you do that for me, please?"

"I'll sure be trying, Mr. Doyle," he answered. The head had not turned. "Yessir, I'll surely *strive* to be as good someday as you was."

"Thank you," I whispered.

Then I gasped and stared as the old man nonchalantly swung open the bent, clattering door on the driver's side; his. The younger man, on the passenger's side, was Orville. I *perceived* that, then, nodding as I learned it. And steadying my former property, the dilapidated old typewriter, in the bed of the truck behind the old fellow and Orville, the machine passed back to him, was the bright-eyed boy named Carlos. I nodded pleasantly some more.

"And I'm Pete," said the aged man at the wheel. That was when he turned his battered old head and his remarkable eyes seemed to see me. "Plain Old Pete."

He *winked*—more or less in my direction.

I came closer in a panic of passion and something akin to mystification. In all the days I could remember I'd never been so damn glad to hear a human voice; because it wasn't in my head, he'd spoken aloud, man-to-man! I put out a trembling hand and realized at once that Old Pete merely *sensed* my presence. He couldn't actually see me.

But it was enough, and I beamed at him, wanting to hug him. Obviously, he was more than a little psychic, probably what parapsychologists might have termed an untrained sensitive. From a foot away, I looked closely at him and then enunciated my own new situation in the manner of a man confiding to a priest: "I'm the resident haunt, Pete."

Whether he'd heard me, I didn't know. I sort of held my breath. Looking exhausted but happy, the old-man-with-my-typewriter perched high upon the driver's seat, a torn cushion under his bottom; and I realized he was the kind of firm, independent fellow who'd sit at the steering wheel of his own truck as long as humanly possible.

He'd made no move toward starting the motor.

Then, slowly, he removed his battered felt hat and rested it in his lap. There was old grease on the brim, I saw, and a rip; the hat was as useless and broken as I, but I noticed an incongruously vivid emerald feather fluttering proudly in the hatband.

"You're a powerful *sad* spook, Mr. Doyle. Ain't that so?" Now the old man's lips did not move. Mind-to-mind, he was transmitting his thoughts. To me. Helplessly, I nodded. "Well, sir, that's an awful shame, a terrible shame. Folks isn't meant to be unhappy when they pass over, Mr. Doyle. They's meant to be in *glory*."

"*Help me, Pete.*" I thought it, said it, *sent* it, a heartfelt plea.

Pete inclined his head; it seemed bent by a great weight. "Used t' know a fine woman, Mr. Doyle, name of Latitude. I reckon she might of helped you—*to go on.*" Blinking, I leaned eagerly against the truck door, hanging on his unfinished speech. "She was a minister, sort of, in her day. And I went with Latitude lots of times, to see her good works. An amazin' soul, Mr. Doyle." Pete sighed. "But Miz Latitude up and died, sir, and now I jest don't rightly know anybody as . . . *special* . . . as she was. Don't know if they's still people like that in this world."

He was crushing my hopes despite his decency and his open, sympathetic heart. I could sense that I was filling him with my grief but I couldn't stop, I had to keep trying. "*Please,* sir," I begged. "*Help* me, Pete. *Somehow.*"

At the instant his physical hand went toward the key in the truck ignition, his internal fingers reached out to touch my mind. They were rough-tipped but gentle. I heard the motor cough, caught a chugging noise, saw there was a coming-to-life of that old pickup which I could never experience. When Pete finally looked my way, his eyes met mine on the empathetic wings of some indescribable, wild old faith.

"Somethin' stands in your path, Mr. Doyle," he said, inside. "I seen such things afore, long years back, with Latitude. Somethin' is *stoppin'* you from advancin', from your right to go on. And I jest ain't no match for powers like that!" He shifted gears, sadly shaking his head. "Truth is, Mr. Doyle, I'm feered you are jest plain—earthbound."

So that was it. I stared at the truck haltingly backing out of my drive, bouncing noisily into the street, and tried again to reach Old Pete's mind with mine. Carefully, quite politely, he'd raised a barrier.

Little Carlos in the back of the truck gave me the impression of looking amiably in my general direction, but I supposed that was wishful thinking. Even if it wouldn't be that exceptional for Pete to leave behind something important, something of his own, in the wide-eyed, handsome head of his grandson. It pleased me when the child raised his hand; but perhaps it was only my imagination that Carlos was waving at me.

Distantly, the truck's horn tooted. I could see nothing in front of it from where I stood. I knew for whom Carlos had intended that last friendly salute. Automatically I lifted my own unseeable hand to wave back at those who might believe but could not help.

Earthbound. The word was paralyzing but I said it aloud anyway, trying to get used to it. *Earthbound*.

When I shook it off and silently followed my widow through the snow, I saw how miserably cold she looked and yearned to hold her.

But she was heading into the house that no longer belonged to me, and neither did she.

We made only one set of footprints.

CHAPTER 7

For a time, Louise Doyle stood at her bedroom window on the second floor, holding back the curtains and looking with sad, troubled eyes at the garage across the lawn. The garage, Zach's loft-den particularly, looked as deserted as a building in a ghost town; it wouldn't have surprised her to see evidence of cold wind whistling through the place. There were no tears in her eyes because she doubted that her ducts had found the spare time to begin making more; by now, she was simply cried out and ready to start putting the pieces of her life back together. One important step had alredy been taken, a secret shared by only one other individual; and she'd explore the possibility if it killed her.

Louise was a very determined woman.

Still, today had been difficult, almost agonizing.

Making the passing of her husband Zach final by means of the especially significant step of removing his most prized, personal possessions had proved far harder than she had expected. Some of the people Louise knew, even members of the family, had been inclined to marvel at the cool composure she'd consistently shown during the months since Zach died. A few of them, Louise sensed, probably thought she was truly a coldhearted wench.

Louise was a very private woman.

None of them knew about her terrible times, alone in the house, when she had dropped what she was doing and rushed upstairs to sprawl upon the bed—*their* bed—and let it all pour out. They didn't know or really want to know what she was truly like, the way Zach had, or how she'd taken his death in the most personal of ways—as an affront, an outrage. It was, in Louise's opinion, conveyed to nobody, a loss which appeared to mock all the effort the two of them had put into this, her second marriage.

Sure, everybody who lost a loved one considered it unfair; somehow it was never the time for a person you adored to die, not even if he or she was one-hundred-and-two, not even if the dying party had been in pain for months. And their views, Louise felt, were entirely right. It never could be the time for a loved one to be processed like a side of cold beef through tradition's bureaucracy, that whole ugly essentially pointless one-more-hole-to-dig-in-the-ground-today-Joe *burying* system, with its built-in obligations to smile when you needed to cry, and cry when you only wanted to be left by yourself.

But in the unexpressed conviction of Louise McIntyre Doyle, everything connected with Zach's dying was unique, and the system, plus the people they'd known and loved, couldn't recognize the fact.

They had thougt Louise and Zachery formed just one more married couple with all the affection steadily eroding, like most people. A couple that tolerated, and excused and probably fooled around on the side, a couple that had managed to weather the trials and tribulations of those first years of so-called wedded bliss, then made a practical accommodation for the good of the kids, the worst excuse of all; or out of mutual detestation of divorce's gross inconveniences; or maybe from sheer inertia. They'd thought Louise and Zach had long ago reached the conclusion of most married folks: that loving was okay for the very young, but that, as the years passed, you put your sensible goals ahead of the snuggly times together. That you either chose the free-spirit getdown cool revolutionary route, trying every drink and drug accessible by even the most illicit of means, or meekly agreed to whatever biased nonsense the stronger set of inlaws foisted upon you. That you held a perpetual open house and welcomed people who, unannounced, dropped by and adamantly refused to see the frigid lump of nervousness knotting behind your eyes. That you talked about your husband or wife behind his or her back, privately loving your best friend much more than you'd ever been honest enough to cherish your mate (even if you *did* groove on it when your friend's marriage was the first in the block to split up). That you were delighted to abandon the carefree, intimate, really *good* times you enjoyed with your mate whenever some bored and loveless jerk had the impulse to telephone, or to pressure you into visiting them (where you would be served an effete, "in" meal and afterward go home to feast lavishly on bacon-and-eggs while you found your *chosen* companion's two-o'clock wit irresistibly funny).

Well, it simply had not been a case of Mr. and Mrs. Doyle, community clones. They'd been through too much together not to appreciate individuality. Proud, her eyes smarting, Louise let the curtain fall back into place and turned to confront her quiet bedroom. Expressionless, she folded her hands in front of her with a gesture like closing a book, and stood there. There was, Louise reminded herself with an effort at a smile, a lot of that going around lately. Standing; or sitting in a chair, staring sightlessly into space; turning off the TV at eleven P.M. (could she know for sure where *her* children were? The voiceover at the start of the Eyewitness News always drove her to check their beds) with the realization and she had no recollection of what she'd seen that evening. *Viewed*, they called what you did with television; people *viewed* TV—and corpses.

There had been all those a lot lately, and nagging. Picking at the boys the way Mother used to squeeze her thumb and index finger together and find fine lint on her school dress, her face fierce with concentration—and, despite herself, bursting into unstoppable tears. She'd let down that much two or three times while Eddie and little Tom looked at her with a puzzled expression she was just now learning to loathe. Oh, it certainly wasn't their fault they were adjusting so inconceivably well; and of *course* she was happy they were putting freshly-gone Zach Doyle in a dusty limbo of their memories along with each season's Hilarious New Sitcoms, cancelled after six weeks.

Louise lowered herself to the bed as if she might be sore, sat on the edge and looked across at the window with the faintly blowing curtains. Neither of her boys saw that it was, in a way, a compliment when doughty, resilient, stiff-upper-lip Mom bawled in front of them. It probably gave her poor munchkins the notion that their real Mom had somehow been replaced by a leaky-eyed bodysnatcher, invading from some subterranean lake. For some reason, it didn't humiliate her to let down around them. After all, they shared her grief, they weren't outsiders.

Were they? All this morning they'd been tumbling on the floor as if they were still three years old, and yesterday they'd slept so late she had finally awakened them, concerned. Louise nibbled on a dry lip. That was the instant she realized she'd made up her mind about it, that Eddie and Tom would have to visit her mother for a few weeks. Not really because they were driving her crazy with their antics, or the way Eddie didn't come home when he'd said, or even the way the two of them tried to engulf every atom of the house with noise from his Ozzie Osborne records and the single Kiss album Tom played over and over. Part of it was that she couldn't stand their adjustment, when hers was so slow, even grudging; part of the reason she wanted them to visit Grandma awhile was because she felt deeply anxious about their activities away from home.

But primarily, Louise wanted the house to herself for awhile. The plan wasn't so much to adjust to Zach's absence, nor even that she was privately considering the possibility of selling the house. In reality, she craved a period of time alone to think about him, intentionally, and consciously, and fully a final time. Let the outsiders go straight to hell if they didn't approve of it. Zach wasn't a mere neighbor, a delivery man, some guy she'd met at a foolish party. He was—or he'd been—the rest of her life.

Because Louise had concluded, at the time when her first marriage fell apart, that it had been mutual selfishness and the constant pressure of chance acquaintances which led to Dick's drinking and carousing. Agreeing to marry Zach, she had determined to blend her interests and aspirations with his to the best of her ability and make it fundamentally unnecessary for him to seek outside relationships of any constant, consuming kind. She'd informed him on their honeymoon that he was free to go where he pleased at night, anytime, then set out to be such a warmly companionable, enjoyable, and supportive mate that the need for other people would not arise.

It had worked; they had been closer and more contented than any couple either of them knew.

But there'd been problems from sources Louise had not anticipated. First, her son Eddie became convinced that Dick was the greatest father in the world, despite the way Dick had headed east without so much as a backward glance or a birthday card or Christmas gift for Eddie. He'd refused to give Zach an opportunity to know and love him the way Louise did, displaying nothing to his stepfather but his worst features. And Zach Doyle, unacquainted with parenting or with the extraordinary ingenuity and willfulness of an energetic young boy had eventually distanced himself from Eddie.

That had been only one stumbling block to Louise's game-plan. After the honeymoon, Zach had made it clear that he wanted desperately to become a successful, published writer. Whether it was his way of saying that he wanted to get *something* out of the unusual family relationship—to make his creative children somehow a match for the running-rampant Eddie—Louise hadn't known. But despite the fact that she had never met an aspiring writer before, she'd done her best to understand and to help. For several years, Zach's singleminded dedication to his craft and his long periods of solitary work were as foreign to Louise's experience as her son Eddie was to Zach.

Into that odd situation had come their son Tom. Almost immediately, Louise's hopes that the new child would improve conditions in the household were dashed in a way she could not have anticipated. Because Zach, loyal to a fault, was so anxious to make Eddie accept him that he steeled himself against showing little Tommy his natural, fatherly feelings. "Nobody will ever accuse me of playing favorites," he said many times to her. "I want Eddie to be my son as much as Tom."

That was, as things turned out, exactly the case.

Neither boy treated Zach as the ordinary Dad he genuinely yearned to be. Instead, as Tom grew, his approach to Zach was a mirror-image of Eddie's. Tom, in effect, chose to be a stepson too. Eventually, the pair of them had become a constant source of irritation and heartache.

Which was the *other* thing outsiders had not known or cared to learn about the Doyles, and Louise's primary realm of pride, of grim satisfaction: because there had never been a resolution, really, of the incessant difficulty with her two boys—never an armed truce, a real meeting-of-the-minds—*but neither Zach nor she had ever seriously considered parting*. Despite the violence produced by Eddie and Tom, despite the fact that they were in debt most of their marriage and rarely able to take in a movie, they'd put their own relationship first and made it *work*. Happy endings, Louise knew, stood a very good chance of occurring only in garish romance novels and afternoon soaps; children did not change their minds, or hearts, overnight, and millionaire publishers did not rap at the door with advances for five hundred thousand dollars. In a wry, hard-to-comprehend fashion, some good fairy waving a magic wand and turning the Doyle household into an idealistic picture might have seemed a contradiction of their day-to-day determination, shared hard luck, their pragmatic acceptance of who they and the boys were—not a validation. All that was drama, not the reality they knew.

But Zach's death at the time when he was finally starting to earn large enough royalties from his books to open up avenues of improvement and pleasure to which they'd never before found access was neither validation nor contradiction.

It was unjust, somehow inane—ludicrous. It seemed to Louise that heaven—nature, faith, God—was denying its own principles of conduct, or system of sacrifice-and-reward. It was, at best, cruel mockery.

And so she needed time to weigh what had happened, to sort things out. Perhaps when she had, she could begin responding in some small and flattering way to the blandishments of Mike Abernethy, the old family friend who so clearly desired to become a different kind of companion.

While the plain black phone on Mother's neatly-ordered telephone stand summoned the woman (Louise could nearly see the scene: white pad firmly affixed to metallic holder, a shiny new ballpoint pen always ready for incoming messages, which seldom came) Louise found her attention straying. She gazed, more curious than frightened, at the areas of her bedroom where she'd become miserably cold of late. It was peculiar. Almost as if some unseen, graveyard ghoul had burrowed up from the basement to give her the fleeting notion that she was . . . haunted. Vaguely, she rememberred when people she'd known had lost loved ones and how they sometimes reported inexplicable little incidents. Doors left ajar; a sounding surf, in homes miles from water; nothing important, really. She wondered if the fact of proximity to the freshly dead bestirred qualities in the living mind which temporarily caused inanimate objects to *move* the way they did in horror movies.

Such things, of course, were positively ridiculous.

Louise turned back to the phone. In her own way, she wanted to be a modern woman, which seemed to her to mean a person who was fundamentally a believer in her own kind, and nothing more. If there was no God, there was no hereafter; if there was no hereafter, there was no such things as a ghost.

But oh, sweet Lord, you must exist, Louise thought with a burst of anguish that made her fingers tighten on the receiver of the phone. She brushed back a lock of hair, wishing passionately she didn't have to phone her mother at all. *I want there to be a God and a hereafter. I want to be with Zach someday.* But there'd been no sign of a cold spot in the bedroom all day, not one.

If Zach had been there, Louise decided sadly, he was gone now.

Mother came on the phone at last and talked non-stop for six minutes. She was a fountain of advice that day, overflowing with an insistance that Louise needed to "put all *that*" behind her, had to "pull yourself together," had to "place the little ones first, and *live* for them—*through* them."

Midway through the conversation, after Mother had agreed to take Eddie and Tommy for an indefinite period of time, Louise stopped listening.

She'd decided to let Mike Abernethy take her out to dinner.

Because human beings neither lived for other people, nor through them, not if they were to remain remotely human, or alive.

It wasn't all the nightmares he'd had for nearly a

year now that frightened the small, charming boy. While he didn't rightly understand at all how they let him look into the future, and it was awful spooky on those apparently ordinary days when his dreams began turning into reality right before his immense, deep-brown eyes, they weren't actually *bad* stuff, terrible things. As a matter of fact, little Carlos couldn't imagine for the life of him why Jesus, or nature, wanted him to dream about future events. Most of them were so boring and unimportant that they weren't worth the bother.

No, what scared Carlos was one nightmare in particular. *The* nightmare. The one he'd been suffering through almost every time he closed his eyelids, since he and Daddy and Grandpa picked up that junk at the Doyle house. *That* nightmare was the worst thing that had ever happened to Carlos, and it kept coming back!

Earlier, he had tried to discuss the subject of his prophetic nightmares with Orville Patterson Hawkins —that was Daddy himself; he'd had Mama stitch the whole name into his work clothes pockets and Carlos thought it looked very fine—and that had been a serious mistake. Daddy, he remembered, had told him almost angrily that it was "all in your imagination, boy," and then muttered about Grandpa Hawkins. Something about him having "no right to fill my boy's ignorant head with sheer nonsense," which didn't make any sense to Carlos. The dreams were real and he adored his old grandfather, understood that the old man regarded himself as a psychic (whatever that was). But Grandpa didn't even know about the look-ahead dreams. That was what Carlos had come to call them, as they recurred almost nightly; his "look-ahead dreams."

Except the awful one about being in the house of those white folks named Doyle, and nearly getting himself killed. That was Carlos' look-ahead nightmare, not dream, and he wouldn't have told Daddy about it for five dollars. Because he had seen the doubting looks exchanged by his parents whenever he tried to explain himself, especially when the topic was something like his bad dreams; and Mama spooked him even more than them, because she got her scary worried-look in her eyes, then made that "tsk-tsk-tsk" sound with her tongue and teeth. Sometimes Mama and Daddy even discussed something called a "shrink," and that truly scared the pee out of Carlos. He was little enough without some mean white man *shrinking him!*

Of late, it had dawned on Carlos that most folks he knew did not have look-ahead dreams or nightmares. They didn't even know how to make pennies jump up from the floor, or get hot, just by looking at them! Only Grandpa could do such things, Carlos supposed. And the only time he'd had the nerve to mention such stuff to the old man, it was on the way home from that Doyle house and Granps hadn't said much about it at all. "You see that white man by the driveway?" he'd asked; Carlos had nodded and told Grandpa he could nearly look right through the stranger. Then old Gramps had said he would be talking with Carlos soon, telling him some things about "the two of us" which Carlos should know.

Teeth brushed, his friendly brown face washed except for behind the ears, Carlos undressed for bed, hoping he wouldn't have the look-ahead nightmare that night.

But he did, and this time it got worse.

Because he saw himself standing *right in front* of the white man whom Carlos knew, now, was a ghost, and the basement door was opening the way it always did in his dreams, and that enormous creature—Carlos knew it was *bad*, the way grown-ups used the word; mean as dirt, a being of evil like the kind they talked about at Sunday School—was down in the basement, looking up the steps at *him!* During the nightmare, until that night, he'd never been able to see any of the Thing's features and the worst thing that had occurred was Carlos *knowing* the Thing was going to get him. Knowing it for a fact, the way he knew his own name.

But tonight was—different.

He saw the monster's pale, pasty, unbelievably ugly face. And he saw what it was going to do when it got him. Because it happened, in the look-ahead nightmare that night—because it opened its mouth bigger and wider than Carlos had ever seen anybody's mouth, and staring down into it was like standing on the edge of an underground cave, peering a thousand-million miles down into the blackness until you thought you saw fires burning, flames leaping, a river of lava swirling through the great stone sides of the hole and shadowing beings with their sizzling feet plunged up to the ankles with the skin boiling right off their bones!

. . . Because Carlos saw those mammoth jaws closing

around his neck, shoulders, and waist, and *felt* the snow-white teeth like stalagmites and stalactites biting deep into his flesh and *meeting* . . .

Screaming, Carlos sat up in bed. His eyelids were batting like flying things trying to take to the air; his heart was also beating like something caged and demanding that it be allowed to leave—to flee the broken, bisected brown body.

Carlos saw where he was—his own bedroom, Daddy and Mama just down the darkened hallway— and pressed his fingers to his mouth to stifle the terrified outcry. He didn't want them to come running, he didn't want to be *shrunk!* That might hurt as much as being bitten in two.

And besides, Carlos realized as he frantically patted his torso to make sure it was intact, he hadn't *died* in the nightmare. Not *yet* . . .

But surely, he prayed, small hands fumbling for the nearby New Testament, surely that wasn't a *look-ahead* nightmare! It couldn't be, it *mustn't* be!

Because if it was, real life was different.

If something bit you into two pieces, you *stayed* that way. Dead.

CHAPTER 8

Suddenly I was sitting up on the cold floor of my garage, incapable of understanding why I could not see clearly. I made a catlike gurgling sound at the back of my throat; the universe appeared to have gone nova and the brilliant explosion of golden light brought my defensive arm before my eyes like neurotic old Bela Lugosi in a Dracula film. The perception that sunshine was blinding me came fast and sensibly enough, but brought with it another sequence of shocks. Because I didn't know whether the sun was coming up, to start the day, or going down to end it.

I realize now that such reactions are commonplace for everybody. But I felt the way a living person feels when his recent sleep was unscheduled or accidental, and he has no idea how long he has been asleep. My sense of panic went on building until it was enough to send the population of a good-sized city screaming into the streets.

Because I'd been "gone" long enough that I didn't even know what *day* it was.

Instantly, the bubbling waters of my fear were smoothed. Simply by wondering—in effect, I guess, by "asking"—I had all the answers to my frightened questions.

I'd been lying in the garage, unnoticed, of course, for almost three days, and the hour was five-oh-one in the evening. Yet sometimes, even for those who are alive, finding the answer to one mystery just turns the page to another set of unpleasant quizzes: because how I acquired knowledge of the time and the date *at once*, without looking at a watch or a calendar, I simply didn't know.

But I also didn't have a shadow of a doubt that I was correct.

For awhile, I sat there in the flush of setting sunlight, my eyes slightly averted, mulling it over. Presumably, since I was dead, I was beginning to have a greater appreciation of the true nature of time. Often, we forget that God did not create the calendar, at least not directly, or command us to measure time by the rising and setting of the sun. God didn't even invent the clock, or the concept of hours and minutes. I remembered something a writer named Richard Heffern had written: "Instinctively I feel that time, like sickness and suffering and evil, was not really meant to be. I do not think that time is an ultimate reality, but rather a part of the human predicament—a part of a confusion and chaos into which we humans are born.

It is a phenomenon that we must ultimately grow beyond, at least in our awareness."

Quite possibly, I thought, time was a predicament one solved, and lost when we humans died; perhaps I was growing beyond it in my awareness. The fact that I had slept, been "gone," suggested some kind of transitory period. I might not need physical nourishment nor even a change of clothes—standing, then, I saw that I had fallen unconscious in a patch of leaked oil, but my garments appeared fresh, even immaculate —but it seemed I still required rest. Periodically, at least. Not that it seemed to be true sleep, because it didn't. Utter dreamlessness, which is to say a complete lack of personal awareness, was part of it. But more to the point was the way I'd slept for days. Never before, in life, had I been able even to remain in bed, dozing, longer than seventeen or eighteen hours, and that was years ago, when I occasionally drank too much.

I could only draw the tentative, working conclusion, just then, that there must be sporadic periods when an enigmatic, possibly unguessable super-nature plainly took over and instructed my poor, battered soul to "get away for awhile." Quite possibly, I saw, to stay sane.

Which thoughts caused me, in turn, to try to inquire more deeply, not without a resurgence of sharp-edged panic, about the universe, the cosmos, and how the Being we called God actually informed and commanded His Place. And it occurred to me that the physiology or pathology, the needs and affairs, even the eventual progress or development of the earthbound dead, might well be under the supervisory direction of a wholly *different* set of so-called "natural" laws. Biology, after all, was the science of *living* things; I existed, yet I did not exist for those with life.

Except, apparently, for an old black junkman.

I found the concept of an alternate nature intriguing, even breathtaking, and began pacing the garage. If there is one kind of physics for the living, but another kind entirely for those who have died and are no longer bound by physical laws, it puts a fascinating and mysterious new face on the whole question of life after death. It opens avenues of inquiry—probably the need for a grand-new approach—that have been explored only by occultists, by metaphysicians. I clapped my hands in excitement. *Of course!* Modern man's scientific experimentation and technologies testing could not, *should* not, be expected to produce proofs of the soul's or personality's survival of death, if the approach depends exclusively upon "facts" and preconceptions that aren't in the slightest relevant: Viewed in that manner, attempting to "explain" all the earnest reports of luminous tunnels and welcoming loved ones furnished by people who had temporarily died was absurd! Why, it was like the old moron joke about losing a dime in the house and going outside to look for it, because the light was better out there!

I remembered reading about the uneducated natives who had not advanced beyond the stone-age and who, finding an airplane landing on their island, drew the conclusion that it was a holy artifact and the "priests" or shamans who flew it were surely gods. We smirk; our superiority laughs at their childlike simplicity. But now I asked myself if they mightn't be close kin to the scientists who, operating from their own limited experience and filled with proprietorial affection for the hard-won facts they'd catalogued, found UFOs landing in their midst plus prehistoric "monsters" in Scottish lakes; footprints of enormous, snowy "missing links"; apparitions of long-dead people who groaned in the night or reenacted events of the dim past—and *also* drew the *wrong* conclusions.

Few "experts"—we use our most complimentary terms so carelessly—denied that people are seeing inexplicable things in the skies, that *something* swims in Loch Ness, that the casts and photographs exist, or that most men and women have seen and heard phantoms for which there is no scientific explanation. Like the savage witch-doctors who argued, at first, against deifying the airplane, it is with the *identifying* of unexplained phenomena that people quarrel. Yet I knew that *I was;* that I *had* survived.

Somewhere along the line, humankind made a list of the Possible, lists of the Impossible, and pronounced them dogma. Yet the Bell Telephone Laboratories ran a computer analysis of many mysterious reports culled by Charles Fort and discovered that frogs falling from the sky did so on exact cycles of 9.6 years! When these cycles were matched against natural events, it was learned that they corresponded to interactions of lunar and solar influences causing great fluctuations in the earth's magnetic field with a precision that, it was also discovered, paralleled an increase in hauntings! Again, I saw, the accepted-natural stood side by side with the dubious-supernatural. Which, again, neatly supported the ancient, eastern acceptance of yin and yang; of opposites permeating all of nature.

Wasn't it, I wondered, wasn't it all a matter of people preferring to accept certain aspects of reality and not others—a question of becoming so biased about the things we wished to believe that anomalies made us fearfully nervous and thus too angry to expand our knowledge as we might?

I lowered my fleshless flanks to the steps leading up to my now emptied garage den, still trying to piece things together. A child believes in God, and perhaps Jesus; in Santa Claus, and—while we do not care to record this fact—in the immortality of his family and of himself. Growing, learning, he is obliged to discard his previous acceptance of jolly old St. Nick, even though society has cooperatively supplied him with considerable evidence: living, plump men with white beards and red suits, packages with Santa's signature, and so forth. Bewildered, obliged to ignore the evidence of his own sight and experience, he reaches eight or ten years upon the planet and is divested of the conviction.

But the same child is encouraged to continue onward with the *former*—belief in God, heaven, hereafter—while each of us strives mightily to retard the time when he must discard the latter; familial foreverness.

And burdened by our well-intended act of apparent kindness, our own grown-up aversion to death, we were forcing him to challenge, in the long run, the single thing he was ever *intended* to believe.

Because the child's initial experience of a grand-parent dying is genuinely shattering. It is unfailingly a contradiction of what he was tacitly, or actively, encouraged to accept. The event casts instant doubt upon his parents' word of common sense, and those of society as a whole, and upon those residual beliefs he had in Divinity and his own immortality. The revolutionary, the assassin, may well be born at just such a time. And then at the very end, aged or ill, being nothing more nor less than a former child, he must give up his conviction about his *own* foreverness. Or so it can be. If he is fortunate, a single sort of faith endures: His belief that there is a God; purpose; goodness; an afterlife.

But I saw clearly then that all the other convictions had been stripped from the ex-child *while he was yet alive*. It was humankind which had created and established all the presumably well-meant myths, the half-truths as well as the lies; they had grown like weeds, willy nilly, again from misconception and the searches for serene fact, launched from a native-island vantage-point of ignorance. And it was humankind which had taken them away, *not God*. In the end, with dying, I realized, resided the potential essence of faith and a great reality. Because the former child whom all of us were might be forced to abandon every unestablishable article of faith during the course of his lifetime, but if he carried away with him *the only belief that mattered*, he would be beyond the grim, glib savagery of human negation at last.

For I *was* dead; I *knew*, now, that only the process of dying could lead to a confirmation of that final belief; and that only on the far side of death waited the absolute verification for which people had sought, had worked and investigated, had fought and died, for thousands of years.

I felt better, then. I felt good, in a way I never had before. If I was an anomaly myself, because I had not been "collected," it still had to mean that millions upon millions of people who were better than I had safely made it to . . . "absolute verification." But I was uncertain where to turn, or what to do next, and only mildly surprised when I saw that I'd totally accepted the evidence of my drastically limited senses: I was dead, definitely, and I would remain that way. There was no lingering doubt; it had all seeped away while I was "gone."

Hearing footsteps outside the garage door, seemingly those of more than one person, I looked up with the unspoken prayer that They had come for me —whoever, or whatever, "They" proved to be.

Angelo stood in the open space, head lowered, sniffing the garage floor.

Then, following as direct a line as if he'd been on a leash, my big St. Bernard dog began walking toward me.

I held my breath. Perhaps there was something behind me, in the corner beneath the steps leading to my study; an old bone, maybe, which he had not been able to bury in the cold, packed earth.

Angelo put his soft, massive, silken head in my face, and a rough tongue came out to lap in the general direction of my right cheek.

Tears in my eyes, I put my arms around his big neck and tried to hug him. Part of my mind warned me, that second, that it would not be possible, that my arms would pass through him as they had Louise's slender waist.

But something happened that I can only classify as a miracle of sorts.

At the instant my unseeable flesh touched his brown fur—or more likely, when Angelo had the blind faith to try licking my face—I *felt* his affable, lumpy old body and I *knew*, without question, that Angelo sensed the affectionate clasp of my arms.

It didn't last. Whatever the nature of the miracle, it was short-lived. But it lasted just long enough for both of us to be sure it wasn't wishful thinking or idle imagination; and when I said huskily, "Good old pal," my dog's humongous rump wriggled with cognizance and delight.

He lay down at my feet, the way he had so often, not being a bother about it but close enough to say, "Hey, boss, I'm here if you wanna romp or feed me or just sit together like a couple of old friends." And I went on feeling better, a whole lot better—so much so that, when my misty gaze rose and fell upon the steps leading to my den, I considered going up and taking a look around.

The only friend I had in the world raised a meaty hindleg to scratch unangrily at a flea—the flea and me; Invisibility Inc.—and I smiled at him. Unhindered by the logic or indoctrination of human thought, his own senses nearer, perhaps, to nature, Angelo's perceptions had adjusted adequately to know I was around. How *fine* that was, I reflected; how *loving!* People went out of their way to find complexities, they manufactured red tape, details, fine print, and doubt, if they didn't discover it upfront.

I leaned back against the step above me, glad to know Louise had sent the boys away to her Mother's. I knew she'd made arrangements in the same way I'd known the day, and the time, and I was learning not to question such information. Certainly I had not gone back to our bedroom and doubted I would. ever. It was miserable enough when we were downstairs and she was fully dressed. Not that it was sex I craved; far from it. I'd never been able to catalogue all there was to love about Louise and, while I was a writer, I wasn't quite compulsive enough to prioritize a list of reasons why I loved her. All I knew was that this aspect of me continued to exist, but Louise didn't know it; and that if she *did* know I was here, it might be possible to form some crazy, otherworldly kind of relationship that would be fulfilling for each of us. Once, I'd spoken with sophomoric sophistication about feeling that people were pawns in a tremendous, cosmic game; but now I found it was actually a case of the dead being pawns of *living people*. It was—

The idea came to me then: Why couldn't I *write* to her?

If she couldn't see, hear, or feel my presence, she could still *read!* Immediately I was on my feet, ignoring Angelo as his huge head raised in sleepy surprise; and I took two steps up the stairs to my den. Surely the three junkmen had left a single pencil, somewhere in a corner—a scrap of old notepaper! And if Angelo could experience my touch, however fleetingly, perhaps I could teach myself to grasp a pencil! The letter

96

wouldn't have to be lengthy, I didn't have to produce it writer-fashion, with style and all the punctuation in the right places because Louise would recognize my handwriting, know I was back!

As I took the third step toward my loft-study, I suddenly felt—there's no other word for it—*beckoned*. That moment my hearing was suffused with the most ineffably lovely music I'd ever heard in my life. Melodically meandering through my mind, serenading my soul itself, it swirled around and within my consciousness and I felt the burdens I'd carried since awakening in my casket lifted lightly from my shoulders. I felt eager, happy, carefree, tried to run—

And saw in my mind's eye an image of Louise, sorrowfully reaching a decision that I knew had already been settled while I slept, but a decision that might be changed—*must* be changed!

She was definitely thinking of selling our house and moving away!

She couldn't! It was *my* house, too. How could I exist with strangers living in the house we'd called our own? How could I remain *sane* if Louise left?

I dashed across the garage and out into the snow, determined to change her mind.

CHAPTER 9

The lividly furious Chauncey Wells, having brushed boldly past the secretarial ogress at the outer desk as if her ocelot eyes hadn't become enflamed with rage and her humpish hackles risen until her face sank mercifully into her rather fleshy shoulders, barged into the sumptuous private offices of Newton Link. He was damned (or given a penance) if he'd wait to be asked in, especially under the present hellish circumstances. Now, Wells' generous features dangerously mottled by ire, he pushed most of his considerable bulk across the dapper Link's impressive desk and was shaking a stout, cautionary finger in the devilishly handsome face. He'd get action on Zachary Edson Doyle today or get reborn trying!

"Hear me out, Link, you bureaucratic bugbear! Enough is enough! There is postively *no provision, no*

Creator's clause or subset styxian codicil, *no* angelic amendment or asmodeustic article, *no* triparite agreement or Hecate's evasion or subsidiary inquisitional covenant, *no* intercessionary response or transdenominational *pact* to allow another unpunished example of your inexcusable, utterly intolerable intervention! I mean it, Link—*this* time it looks like the Second Coming, for sure!"

"Oh, brother," Link said mildly, sounding epicenely weary. "My good soul, it is much too sulphurically steaming this busy morning for one of your justifiably famed, righteous tantrums! The air conditioning is down again this week and all the repair men I might otherwise spare are roasting on a spit! Standard regs, and you know how *that* is. Come, do be a good fellow and explain yourself—or even better, send down one of your reconstituted cherubim with the lusty cheeks; they just might get some air circulating in here!"

Still hellbound after weeks of mutually tracking the activities of Zachary Doyle's spirit and futilely negotiating for an early paradisical release (an EPR), Wells found himself longing for the moderate northern clime. This place was the pits, and the latest sequence of moral outrages was plainly too much when even Newton Link considered it too hot. Thinking about the games and the nymphs of the Elysian fields, or the famed fantasy-fountains at Eden, was virtually a mortal sin for an angel in his condition. "You already *have* every repair man, furnace person and chimney-sweep, every *concierge* and landlady and slumlord, on the other face of the world," Wells protested. "But don't try your evasive tactics on me, Newton. It won't work this time!"

Link, who had done his best to seem at a loss to comprehend this intrusion of his opposite number, merely offered Wells a sympathetic shrug. "I'm afraid you have me at a disadvantage, Chauncey. Judging from your bulging bishop's eyes and that cardinal's complexion, I'd almost think you were seeking a transfer."

"If I ever get you at an *ideal* disadvantage, sir, you'll certainly have good reason to be afraid!" The heavenly emissary squeezed his eyes shut to keep the fury contained, dutifully counted to ten amendments, and settled heavily into a chair. It wouldn't do to permit his understandable sense of injustice to eclipse the reason for his visit. "I am thinking, Newton, about the underhanded manner by which you influenced Zachary Doyle's widow Louise to hire three men to clean out the spirit's study."

"Oh, that." Link shrugged.

"Yes, *that!*" Wells snapped. "D'you really believe I'm so naive that I failed to see the handicap you devised for us?"

"Well, one can hope," Link replied. His smile was dazzling. "Why don't you explain my insidious device? Humor me."

"I mean," said Wells, leaning forward, "that with all his most prized possessions removed from the study above the garage, the poor soul has no reason left to go up there!"

"Very good, old man," Link murmured. "I really didn't think you saw that one." He leaned forward, too, all blandness wiped from his face. For an instant, the wink of an eye, he'd allowed Chauncey Wells to see his real features and it was an unsettling glimpse, even for an angel. "We were merely preventing your people from placing us in check, Chauncey. *You* instigated this fresh series of unregulated affronts when you cancelled the defensive spiritfield around the Doyle house. Obviously, your ardent little prayer was that he would leave the place and wander up to his den. What d'you call that, old upholder of the faith? Fighting fire with fire?"

"Do we have any other choice," demanded Wells, "until my Head decides simply to eliminate this damnable abyss from the cosmos? It was *your* side which stopped Doyle's spirit from mounting those steps this very evening!" He shook his head and several chins vied for a new position. "How much lower can even *you* get than involuntary telepathy? *Forcing* the poor wraith to see what his widow was planning, indeed!"

"It wouldn't have been necessary," snapped Link, the claws on his fingers biting into his palms as he knotted his fist, "if *you'd* refrained from planting the idea of a letter to Louise in his mind!"

Wells' mouth opened in surprise. "I had nothing to do with that."

"You didn't?" Link studied the other, narrowly. "Hm-m. I'm rather a good judge of untruths and dissembling—took a course by that name shortly after arriving here, as a matter of fact; the instructor was a former senatorial candidate—and you seem to be speaking the truth."

"Could I be doing anything else?" asked Wells,

spreading his hands. His almost-golden brows formed a frown. "If memory serves, Link, Doyle himself was running through a number of interesting conjectures. But one matter continues to plague him. Did you notice?"

Link's eyes narrowed. Wary now, he pressed his hands together, fingertip to fingertip. "As a matter of sheer fact, I did." He paused. "Do you allude to the question of where he *goes* when he falls asleep?"

Wells snapped his fingers. "I *thought* you knew something about that!" he exclaimed, trying to cross his legs. He gave up after the third attempt. "There isn't a lot of precedence for the soul-stranded, as we've both remarked. But I didn't think that sort of thing was status quo. Where do you take him, Link? What do you *do* with him?"

"Don't be an infinite ass, man!" Link growled. "It's all very well and good to make idle threats about a Second Coming, but we're both aware it's only rhetoric. Unless my Company or I had the temerity to break the basic, binding rules and throw us all into unscheduled Armageddon."

Wells didn't reply at once. Risking the exposure of a rare skill he'd developed only a couple of hundred years ago, he fixed his gaze on Newton Link's unseen pineal gland and performed a hypernormal scan. "I'm not a bad judge of lies and dissembling myself, old man," he said deliberately, "and I believe you're telling me the truth. Then . . . *who?*"

"Good question," Link retorted. He reached out to the computer on his desk and busily began punching buttons. "I have suspected for some time, brother

Wells, that something extraordinary has come up. I want to check it out—it'll take a few days, I fear—but I can put my theory to you in plain enough terms." He finished programming the device with a flourish and, looking over at his angelic opposite, could not conceal a glimmer of apprehension. "Wells, this may all be hogwash. Bear that in mind, all right? But I have reason to wonder if our time-honored Companies don't have . . . *competition.*"

"A *third* Agency?" Wells asked incredulously.

Link nodded firmly. "And you know what ABC did to CBS and NBC," he added. "But it's no more than a supposition at the moment, my dear fellow—a premise to entice Our Lady of IBM."

"You're a sick spirit, Link," Wells rejoined with a scowl. "And I think you're stalling. I'll never see a shred of evidence establishing the existence of fresh competition. The concept is ludicrous, even—despite your secondary status by unavoidable presence—barely sacrilegious."

"When you're second," said Link, smirking, "you try harder. I wonder what a new nirvanistic network would do to your, ah, cosmic ratings."

"I'll tell you this." Wells arose, the job done in meaty segments until he towered over his seated counterpart. "Because of your incessant intervention, Newton, I am seriously considering permitting Louise Doyle to sell her property—*quickly.*"

"You cannot," Link replied at once. He stood, the picture of confidence, and breeding. "Should that occur, there'll be no reason for the spirit of Doyle to stay. And then *nobody* will claim him."

"Precisely!" Chauncey Wells presented a sublime smile. "That is what I am prepared to do if you mingle in their private affairs to the slightest degree from now on."

Link's return smile was impish. "Then think of this, old soul. The widow is a charming creature. Personally, I find her fleshy attributes altogether enticing."

"You wouldn't!" exclaimed Wells, turning pale.

"Oh, probably not, I'll grant you that!" Link laughed, slapped Wells on the back rather more sharply than camaraderie allowed, and showed him to the door. "It might make both our legal departments exceedingly litigious. But even *there*, I believe, we continue to enjoy a numerical advantage." He opened the door, unable to hide the lust in his blazing black eyes. "And it would be delightful to lure Mrs. Doyle into the basement for a bit of a romp. Fresh blood, and all that!"

Chuckling, he saw the revolted Wells glaring at him as he shut the door in his ample face.

He opened it again, moments later, and peered out into a waiting room hazy with smoke. "Ah, Miss Moloch?" he called, arching one brow and waggling a summoning finger. "Would you be bad enough to come into my chambers a moment? I'd like you to take some . . . *dictation*."

CHAPTER 10

"What are you looking at?"

A pause. "Just checking the weather. More snow comin'."

"No, you're not." Alma Jo gave a hard look at her husband. Even seated, her sleek, willowy legs indicated her height. The fact that she didn't always change her stylish dresses after coming home from a day of modeling stressed the fact that she was working, and he was not. "You're watching Carlos again."

Orville let the curtains fall back into place. Slowly turning away from the window, he made an effort toward erasing the guilt from his face. "Well, why'd you ask me, if you already knew the answer? She-*it!*"

She closed her copy of *Essence*, resting it on the end table beside her chair. "What crazy thing was Carlos doing this time?"

He pretended not to hear her, frowning. "Anything wrong with a daddy keepin' one eye on his little boy?" Orville returned to his chair in the front room across from her and dropped into it hard. "He won't even be ten years old for another couple of months. All kinds of things might happen to him while he's playing."

"I asked you what he was *doing* in the yard?"

"Nothing. Nothing much." Put-upon, Orville retrieved his newspaper from where he'd left it, on the floor. He glanced at the blank-faced TV in the corner, then opened the paper to the sports section and hid behind it. "He was just playin', Alma Jo. Just playin'."

"Liar." She spoke the word softly with the faintest, carrying inflection of old affection, enough for Orville to hear both that and the fact that she was onto the two males. "Orv, he was doing those . . . *strange things* again, wasn't he? Causing the leaves to rustle or fall, or making pennies dance on the sidewalk?" Abruptly she leaned out to him from her chair, a note of rising hysteria in her throaty voice. *"Tell me what you saw."*

Orville lowered the newspaper, his handsome, mustached face pained. "Well, first off, he wasn't makin' no leaves fall because it's winter, remember?" He felt her maternal apprehension and blinked. "You know that snowman he made yesterday? I helped him, remember? Nice old snowman." He saw her nod. "He's melting it."

Alma Jo jumped up. "He's playing with matches and you're just *letting* him?" She started toward the front door. "Honestly, Orville, there are times when I think you're the most irresponsible man I ever—"

"There's no matches." Something in his voice stopped her but she didn't turn. "No lighter, Alma Jo; no fire of any kind except what's *inside* him." He stood, hesitantly crossed the floor toward her. He tried to keep the fear out of his voice. "Sugar, he's melting that snowman . . . *with his eyes.*"

"What?" she asked faintly.

Nodding, he put his arms around her. "Carlos is just *lookin'* at it, and the fire's *within* him." He cleared his throat. "I saw him doing it, Alma Jo. He'd been calling to those kids down the street, the little white boy and girl. Trying to get them t' come play with him. But they acted like they didn't hear him; their momma probably told them not to. And Carlos just sagged. You know, at the shoulders; the way old folks get sometimes. Then he kind of trudged over to the snowman we made." Orville hesitated, and Alma Jo, turning in his strong arms to see his expression, realized he was witnessing the scene again in his troubled thoughts. "Carlos' back was to the house but I saw him double up like fists, straighten his spine, and brace his legs in the slush; then he dropped his chin forward, to concentrate. Like Oscar or Bailey or Wee Willie back in Coach Crowe's day, fixin' to shoot the winning free throw. Well, there was this weird, distant *sound* . . . and the snowman's wide face began to *run*. A carrot we'd used for a nose just tumbled out —and then I noticed something funny, Alma Jo." He looked into her disturbed eyes, clearly frightened. "That carrot looked the way one does when you've over-cooked 'em, *roasted* them—like it was wrinkled up, and *browning.*"

"We have to get help for him—now!"

Orville felt her tugging free of his arms. He held tight, wanting to finish. "Honey, you called out to me and I stopped watching then. But before I glanced away, there wasn't nothing left of that old snowman's head." His expression begged her to believe him, or to make him believe it fully himself. Yet there was an odd sort of pride, too, in his eyes. "Carlos just *stared* at it till it melted into *nothing.*"

"Mrs. DuBois' girl had some problems last year and she mentioned the name of a psychiatrist. I'm going to phone him tomorrow," Alma Jo announced firmly, and this time she did pull away. She strode halfway toward the dining room, where the telephone was, as if hoping to make tomorrow come at once. "I know how your daddy feels about this and all the things he told you about himself since you were little, too."

"Sh-h!" He gestured, pointed to the ceiling. "Old Pete's asleep upstairs right now!"

She whirled, pleading with Orville. "Sweetie, this isn't that terrible, hateful, superstitious south your daddy loved so much! People don't believe in nonsense like that these days. People don't *do* weird things like that!"

"No, they do other weird things instead," Orville replied soberly. He moved quietly toward his wife. "Like attacking old ladies, cuttin' up children and stuffing them into drawers. Honey, it wasn't just the stories Old Pete told. I saw with my own eyes some of the marvelous things he could do—and that magic-woman he knew, Miz Latitude."

"'Magic-woman,'" she scoffed. "Can't you hear what you're saying?"

He gripped her arms tightly, but refrained from hurting her. "I wasn't brought up the way you were, baby. Like you were special, or white or something. I got to see what some folks can do with the power of their *minds*. See, when you're dirt poor, the way my daddy was—the way I was, while I was a boy—you get closer to nature, to the *really* old ways. 'Dirt in your nails fills your mind with the earth,' Old Pete told me." He stopped, relaxed his grasp. "Our Carlos has just got some of the old ways, those abilities, from his Gramp. That's all."

She was worried enough that frustration turned to mounting ire. "But *you* don't have those powers, Orville," she snapped, accusingly. "*You* don't have *any* kind of power!"

"No, ma'am." He simply looked at her. "I guess I don't. I can't make pennies dance on a sidewalk or read people's minds. Hell, baby, I can't even find a *job*." He went to the door then, meaning to call Carlos into the house. "My brain ain't full of earth-magic, just *needs*. Nothin' fancy, like modeling."

"I am going to call that shrink, Orville!" she cried, tense behind him as he tugged open the front door and felt the blast of biting, winter wind. "I'm going to make an appointment, and take Carlos for an examination, and spend some of my own hard-earned money to make sure my only baby doesn't turn into some kind of God-forsaken freak!"

Orville glanced tiredly back at her. "There are no

freaks around here, woman," he said bitterly. "Just poor folks tryin' to get along."

When he looked out front to call Carlos, he saw the boy slumped on the curb, the curve of his small spine the definition of wistfulness. And Orville saw that the snowman he'd built with his son was gone, as if it had never existed.

And half the snow that had covered the front hard had melted as well. Bare, brown, packed earth lifted tufts of sick-looking grass; and his boy was silently eating a carrot.

The eighty-year-old man lying motionlessly in bed on the second floor had no idea that he and his grandson were the topic of concerned, emotional discussion. He also did not really know that he was eighty years old because the southern county into which he'd been born had not kept accurate records of black births. Later, Pete had suggested to his first wife with a wry grin that he supposed the failure to register his beginning in life was pure wishful thinking. If The Man did not write it down, somewhere—if he refused to record the fact that X-number of black children came to earth at a given period—he could pretend to himself that the whites continued to outnumber the blacks. Till they had all grown up, of course, when The Man started feeling he was swallowed up by black bodies. Eventually, things being what they were, he'd be very sure to register the passing of each black with astounding accuracy and more than a little grinning relish.

In Pete's case, his momma had died in childbirth and he'd spent so much of his first ten years or so of life with families other than his real one that the strangers didn't know his birthday, and never thought to ask. Consequently, Pete had never learned the date either; so that, when he'd concluded he was grown up, it had appeared natural to celebrate his natal day whenever he felt that he needed one. As a boy, there'd been times when he enjoyed birthday parties two or three times a year, and reckoned that he claimed more daddies than anybody else in the whole world. And aunts; and half-brothers, half-sisters, second cousins. Which wasn't the most terrible thing that might have happened. Afterward, there was always a "family" Pete could visit—another home—regardless of where he found himself.

And it was during those now-distant days that he'd met an extraordinary lady who called herself Miz Latitude, and learned that he could do naturally some of the bizarre things *she* could do.

Two years ago, when he'd been telling folks he was sixty-nine and had been reasonably sure he was lying, Pete had suffered a spell or two of dizziness. Which was when he'd decided to go ahead and celebrate his eightieth birthday—and a very pleasant occasion it had been, too!

But Old Pete wasn't sleeping while his son and daughter-in-law discussed him and Carlos. He'd been busy, actually—busy "travelin'," as the old man called it. There was no need for a person to spend a lot of money taking expensive trips to exotic places, in Pete's view. Not when you could rest your eyes and your aching back and go just about anywhere you pleased. There'd never been any "Step to the rear of the bus" with Old Pete's "travelin'." It didn't cost a cent. And, just by wanting plainly enough to do it, he'd seen practically every place worth seeing.

He was just returning from his travelin', well-rested and stretching and feeling his warm little lump of soul settle snuggly back into his body, when he discovered that someone else was traveling, too—a much farther piece than Old Pete had ever cared, or dared, to go.

Because Miz Latitude was taking shape at the foot of his bed.

She wasn't doing it all at once, like a lightbulb being turned on. She was kind of *materializing* and, in the shadowy bedroom, she was particularly visible. At first she was just a zillion sparkling dots and dashes gleaming the way they did it on the television, in science fiction shows Pete considered ridiculous. Maybe she was coming in slowly like that, fine-tuning herself, to prevent him from having another heart spell and dying on the spot.

But she still gave him a good turn. Not because he was foolish enough to be fearful—ghosts were just ex-people, no better and not worse than they'd been alive —but because he hadn't seen Miz Latitude since she died and hadn't thought he would until *he* did. He hadn't summoned her, either; although he recollected, as he watched her get clearer and clearer, something she'd told him, long years back: that if he ever believed he saw a spirit but couldn't make out the features too well, he should whisper, "Miz Latitude? That you?"

He got himself propped on his elbows, squinting straight ahead of him. "Miz Latitude? That you?"

It must have helped her, somehow, because the face

sort of hovering over his feet—parchment-featured, so sallow it seemed Oriental, the eyes tiny nuggets of coal that were lost in the bins of her fleshiness—produced a hideous smile. Pete smiled right back at her; he'd have known that leer anywhere, because it was the way Miz Latitude had looked at him when he was around nineteen years old and she was . . . a good deal younger than now. Then her voice reached his ears, appearing to roll upon unseen hillocks of air, powerful but husky. She said, "Pete, you got to mind what I say! That boy needs your protectin'!"

"Carlos?" he asked, forcing the name out.

"Well, who *else*?" The apparition planted fists upon its ample hips, clucked at him for his nonsense. "He's one of ours, old man. Flesh of our psychic flesh! And he loves you."

"Shit, woman, I know that!" Pete muttered. Miz Latitude still hadn't changed. "Is it that dead white man I was talkin' with? Is *he* the danger?"

"He is," she replied, nodding. "He's not there and he isn't here. And he's in bad trouble, Pete, just in time for it to get worse!"

"So you want me to keep Carlos away from him, is that it?"

Miz Latitude's eyes snapped, just the way they used to, except something very much like genuine lightning leaped from them now. Then, to the old man's surprise, the anger went out and a softness he hadn't seen before worked its way across her face. She was pretty! He'd known this woman almost fifty years and he'd never had a glimpse of the way she must have been as a girl. "Lord, honey," she chided him, "you *know* that's

115

not the way it can be! The boy must do what he has to do and that's for certain. I said he was our flesh, didn't I?"

Pete glanced away. It was downright peculiar, but the old woman's light was more blinding when she let her kindness show through. "I should explain things to Carlos, then," he said slowly, understanding. "What it's like to be the most ordinary thing in the world, and the most special, all at the same time. How it's the Lord's purest gift and we got to use it to help those who are special first, and *then* ordinary. But I got to take care of Carlos and maybe even Mr. Doyle. That what you mean, Miz Latitude?"

"Bless your heart, Pete, bless your heart." Her face loomed above his, the sweet smile still in place. "You always was my favorite, you old rascal."

He closed his eyes to accept the kiss, something he'd never have done when she was alive; and when he finally opened them again, she was gone.

CHAPTER 11

The terrifying possibility that my wife Louise would sell our house, and leave it forever—truly leaving me stranded—obliged me to run faster than I ever had in life. With less noise created by my streaking body than would have been caused by the slightest gust of wind, I sped from the garage and burst through my front door.

But odd things, actual and discernible small alterations, and ideas I had never seriously considered before, kept occurring to me, even in that quick passage of time. Possibly most of the changes, that day, were only in the realm of thought and imagining; I couldn't really tell.

Yet I had the powerful impression that I did not actually *have to run*, in order to face Louise and attempt to reason with her; that, if I could seize control of my runaway feelings and stop flying into a panic, I might sort of *will* myself to be transported from the garage to our front room.

For the first time, while my unseen legs churned, I discovered that the concept of finding and using abilities that were beyond the capacity of living men wasn't all that unpleasant. It could, I saw, be taken as evidence of fair play and balance of compensation. Why shouldn't I accept any opportunity for a bit of fun, a sense of fulfillment? I remembered thinking—yeah, I'm aware that this is a great deal to have passed through my mind in such a short span of time; that's part of the point I'm trying to record—that living people complained constantly about their daily chores, whatever the nature of them; but that a real sense of dignity, self-worth, and accomplishment was otherwise impossible. During times of depression and recession, when people were laid off from their jobs, the best of them attempted to find replacement work and I'd always suspected it wasn't just the money. They could not remain idle, as I was now, and maintain a belief in their personal value.

I noticed as I ran, that I could not hear my own footsteps nor, of course, my own hastier breathing because there either was nothing substantial left of old Zach Doyle, or *all* that remained was the substantial part.

And when I arrived at the front door, it was again with the impression that I could pass directly *through* it, if I wished. But despite a variety of evidence supporting that notion, I couldn't bring myself to try—not yet. Hollywood had done enough B movies about ghosts during the forties to make walking through walls a cliche; besides, Houdini did it better anyway. I guess I possessed just enough self respect to dislike the notion of being trite on top of everything else! Happily, the door was open anyway and, as I stepped inside, my last unusual thought occurred to me—that by practicing, I might be able to *will* doors to open, windows to rise, and that I even had within my power then the latent ability to move and manipulate almost *anything* I chose, merely by commanding it.

Then I saw Louise seated on the couch across from the door and temporarily forgot everything I had just experienced.

She looked beautiful, younger and healthier than she'd appeared in years. That was good, because I was the only one who knew she had a minor heart condition and needed to take good care of herself. God knows that the period after my death must have been crammed with tension for her, an awful time of trial; but it looked now like she had decided to put an official end to her mourning.

Because seated on the couch beside Louise—hell's bells, *pressed* against her side, as tightly as he could get without going all the way—was our old family friend of the family and my very good, devoted, all-the-way-back-to-high-school buddy, the lawyer Mike Abernethy. And thus it was that a cliche was forced upon me against my will, since friends of the family who *aren't* are a commonplace in literature. I can only report what happened.

And it may be very important to record that my perceptions, apparently, were going on being sharpened, or heightened, even at times which I saw as crisis periods. If I'd been alive instead of dead, I might have thought—*preferred* to think—that Mike was simply fooling around. Harmlessly, that is. I'd have charged across the floor to grab his hand and shake his arm as if I was trying to pump water.

But dead, a ghost, I knew damned well—at once—that Mike Abernethy had something else in mind.

I'd known that lanky, stiff-spined, bespectacled turkey half my life and always understood that beneath his superficial veneer of politeness and a stuffy habit of censoring his own conversation, was a total stuffed-shirt. Well, I'm putting that a trifle harshly, I guess, because of what I was that evening, and what I had to listen to. Actually, Mike had an entertaining sense of humor. He could be downright witty, when he wished to be; but because he cleaned-up every quip he'd made up or joke he told, his delivery made his humor far funnier than it actually was. What you noticed first about him, if you were old enough to remember, was that he looked a great deal like that actor who'd played the father of "Dennis, the Menace" on TV. Mike had those huge, horn-rimmed specs that gave you the notion he'd had them tailor-made in order to look like a cross between a bug-eyed owl and a starving crane.

What I'd never known, until I found that I could read snatches of his thoughts, was that priggish and pedantic Mike Abernethy had made it with the wives of half the guys he knew. I also discovered that he'd never scored with Louise, or even come close, but that he meant to, that she was uncertain, lonely, and I was out of the way.

Later, with more "mature" thought (a euphemism for "after you've cooled down"), I tried to tell myself that I didn't blame him. From his standpoint, that of the living, I'd been Out of It for months, long enough that he was neither behaving improperly nor trying to turn me into a cuckold. While Louise wasn't every man's cup of tea—she tended, I knew, to polarize opinion—to those men with tastes similar to mine, she had greater beauty and depth of intellect and personality than empty-headed little darlings, pert, busty, long-legged beauties whose attraction ceased two minutes after they'd been bedded. Louise was a woman for the long haul, a permanent kind of person; and that's the reason why I failed, even at a later date, to forgive Mike. I knew what he was thinking and nothing about Mike Abernethy's plans or desires extended much farther than a week.

They had dinner together, Louise clearly (to me) uncomfortable and flustered, behaving absolutely unnaturally; but Mike did his stiff-necked best to be charming, helpful, and irresistible. On Louise's part, I knew that dating another guy, even someone she'd known for a long while, found her rusty, all the girlish coquetries and subtleties long since eliminated by our own total candor with one another. Where Mike was concerned, I began to find it amusing, in a way, because he did not think of himself as a marauding male letching after every heartsick female, the way I saw him. Mike saw himself as a well-meaning nice guy, still a friend of the family, proper, even religious (he went to church at least one Sunday a month), and basically as beneficial for my widow as a bank full of bucks. He kept his lust buried under layers of such self-delusive bullshit and I saw, from my unique vantage point, that the fellow's hypocrisy was absolutely the smartest thing about Mike. With it, he functioned efficiently as an attorney, did little charitable things such as coping with clients from whom he had no reasonable chance of a fee and supported a wife who adored him and three kids who were patterning their lives after the guy. Without it, I learned with amazement, Mike was a beast.

This shouldn't sound like sour grapes. I'm telling you the truth of what I experienced as they dined, murmuring together about old times the four of us (including Mike's wife Cherlyn) had known, sipping wine he'd brought, slipping back into the living room and getting even closer together on the couch. Because I amused myself, if that's the right term, by sifting through the old frustrations and losses in Abernethy's essentially dishonest mind, failures he couldn't admit to himself, lost opportunities he had disguised in self-serving terms such as "looking out for *numero uno*," mistakes of judgment that appeared hideously transparent in retrospect, images of women whom he'd taken at vulnerable moments and the way he'd nice-guyed them into keeping still; and I saw that the unhappiness of Mike's life had constantly fueled his rather primitive, buried lust until nothing but his own priggish self-image prevented him from terrible acts of brutality. I saw that the real Mike, down deep, was no longer the amiable, square kid I'd known in school but something fundamentally monstrous, held in check—

leashed—by nothing more than the glossy, almost wistful picture he preferred to have of himself.

And what would happen, I wondered, if things worsened in Mike Abernethy's life and his options were again changed? I tried to decide if my good old pal was typical of other men, possibly even *most* modern men. You hear about some of them, now and again—businessmen who headed the Jaycees and siphoned away thousands while bridges collapsed. Local bankers who kept pretty, younger women on the side and beat them to death. Taxi drivers and factory workers and congressmen and entertainers who, when the police came, displayed collections of unspeakable things. I wondered if society, in whatever scapegoat combinations you cared to indicate, had done such things to *all* of us and that, like my friend Mike, we stopped ourselves from covert cruelties and craziness only because we liked to think of ourselves as the White Hats, and Good Guys and Girls.

"Zach was the finest man I ever knew," Mike said, "in most respects."

I tensed, stopped ruminating to listen.

"He thought a lot of you, too," Louise replied. Good old Louise, I thought, she didn't fall into the trap!

"But he had his faults," my lifelong friend added, needing no coaxing. He didn't speak any louder. He didn't need to. He had his arm around her shoulders and his head back, as if relaxed, as if he didn't require defanging. "I remember the way Zach had of giving the impression that he knew everything."

"Sometimes," Louise said thoughtfully, "I thought

he did." She was sitting up straight with her feet on the floor like a good girl, arms folded, her gaze vaguely but definitely fixed on a corner of the front room.

"Oh, don't get me wrong!" Mike laughed, his hand squeezing her shoulder. "Zach was exceptionally smart. If he wasn't writing, hard at work, he was reading—improving himself. Sometimes, though, I felt he was inclined to take you for granted, Lou. You must have had to raise the boys virtually without Zach's help."

Knowing Louise despised being called "Lou," I waited eagerly to see how she'd handle this. "Zach never really understood small children," she said, at last. The words crawled through her lips like ugly things escaping. "He could be so stern with them, I was generally glad that he was over in his den." She'd always told me that, since I was conveniently near the house while I worked in my garage loft, she felt we spent more time together than other couples. She paused, glanced at Mike. It must have been a super close-up of his right eye behind the mammoth lens. "Zach didn't read to improve himself but to keep up, for professional reasons. He'd have considered it pompous to read for improvement; like showing-off. Some people don't understand that a man can read, too, for sheer enjoyment, even with thirty or forty television networks available."

"*I* read, Louise," he replied stiffly. "When I have the time."

"Zach always said a person makes the time for what he really cherishes." Abruptly, she laughed and gave him a little shoulder-nudge. That motion of hers always made me feel so special; among many other motions. "I didn't mean to hurt your feelings, Michael. You're the nicest person I know, now that Zach's gone."

Inwardly, I cheered. I could have done it openly, I suppose, since they wouldn't have heard me, but I hadn't accustomed myself yet to being a mute. Louise had timed her comeback beautifully, repaying Mike for calling her "Lou" be referring to him as "Michael." I knew that was a crotchet of his. Then she'd further weakened him by praise.

So why was he getting by with taking her into his arms and kissing her?

I waited for her to break the clinch, my feelings so completely beyond description that I won't try to present them. She did, of course; but not nearly soon enough for me. When she leaned away from him I saw clearly a certain individualistic gleam Louise gets in her eyes when she is physically aroused, and I wanted to throw my good old pal out of the house more than I'd ever yearned for anything before.

But I didn't, of course, because I could not. Nor did I strike him, or try to pull her away, or reach for something to batter them both with at the moment when they arose from the couch, hand in hand, and started up the stairs to our bedroom.

It hadn't happened quickly, let me make that clear. My wife is no pushover. And you shouldn't think she is, simply because she took Mike to bed at the end of their first evening without me. After all, she'd known Michael Abernethy since a few days after she and I began dating—I'd suggested a doubledate, with Mike's wife Cherlyn as the fourth, of course; it had seemed to be the most natural thing in the world, to want my best friend to meet the woman I loved—and *she* couldn't see the wormy, knotted smirk of illicit lust squirming around inside him when he urged her toward the stairs. He'd told her that Cherlyn and he were separated now, getting a divorce. He'd stressed the loneliness that he and Louise felt, the way life had pulled a dirty trick on both of them and that they had a right—*no*, an *obligation!*—to seize a few moments of happiness, and that he'd always love the memory, the way Louise did, of Zachary Edson Doyle.

"Sleeping with my wife isn't my idea of a goddamned *tribute*, you son of a bitch!" I shouted, racing after them. "Give me a minute—I'll think up a better memorial!"

Neither of them heard me, of course. And at the top of the steps, when they turned in the direction of the bedroom, I paused for a moment, wondering if I were going stark, staring mad. A husband might very well want his widow to "find new happiness," as the soaps put it, to "Find someone who can be as dear to you as I." But he wasn't supposed to have to watch it happen! He wasn't supposed to learn that his best buddy was a skirt-chasing bastard who hid his covert desires under a maddening guise of "ending your loneliness!"

By the time I was in motion again, I didn't know whether I was madder than I was disappointed in both of them, or more disappointed and hurt than I was embarrassed to be exposed to their naked needs.

Then they were walking into our bedroom—*my*

room—and, as I barged across the hallway meaning to get their attention somehow, the door was closed squarely in my face.

I think that's when I started sobbing, and slipped to my knees. I decided that I'd had it, all the way; that both heaven and hell had forsaken me.

And I know that's when I went a little mad, and began to do the awful things I did.

CHAPTER 12

The extremely old and the very young, the junkman Pete and his grandson, Carlos, had sneaked out of the house tonight and into the old man's truck, going for a treat.

Several miles away, the ghost of a decent enough white man haunted his own house and, in his misery, began taking spectral steps that would make this the old man's final treat.

It began harmlessly enough. Carlos, during supper, had picked absently at his food and Pete was pretty sure he knew what was disturbing the boy: stray feelings and more-or-less adult impressions which radiated from Orville and Alma Jo. Old Pete had sensed them too; worrisome moods that made a sensitive boy wonder if he'd become a problem to his folks just be living, and if he'd turned into something their neither understood nor approved. Recalling that Carlos adored the roastbeef sandwiches at the neighborhood Arby's, Pete had crippled the spine of a piggybank with two blows of his shoe. He'd been feeding the pig change for years; now it was time the silly thing fed people. He left the remaining two dollars and change in the glass where he usually kept his false teeth and, with his grandson, slipped out of the house.

There were matters for him to discuss with Carlos. Important things which Orville and his woman wouldn't understand. Because there was a whole lot of ways for folks to be earthbound.

Now grandfather and grandson were comfortably seated on the front seat of the truck, Pete's last possession, cozy and companionable. Since it was winter, and cold, Pete let the clackety motor run and kept both windows down an inch. Oily smells from the protesting engine mingled with the fragrance of sandwiches and french fries, and other odors only Pete could smell: furniture of every variation, fitting every shape and need of man; reeking refrigerators; toasters, washers and dryers; mattresses and beds bearing the bitter traces of old love. He'd carried away, in the back of that truck, an uncountable array of articles symbolizing the changes and losses, the steps up and falls down, of enough people to have populated the town if they'd all remained alive. It was a Memory Van, to Pete; he'd considered his truck that for ages without telling a soul. Folks had entrusted the remnants of their past to a smiling old man who, when there'd been time, had touched the discarded memories with both his fingers and his gentle mind.

Here, in this highchair, little Mary and Charlie had perched above the dining table; but they were grown now, and gone to find highchairs for their own children. There, nodding as he touched it, the TV grandma had kept in her silent house; he could almost make out that last show she'd seen.

He'd parked his Memory Van in the shadows behind the fast food restaurant, a time-honored pleasure of Old Pete. Here, unseen, it was possible to practice, to keep in telepathic shape, by gently probing the thoughts of the customers entering the place. Although, he had to confess to himself, there wasn't a lot on their minds these days and even less that separated one person from another. Just a whole bunch of worry over money, the devil's currency; that, and the private hungers and cravings folks tended to have in their heads whether it was 1915, 1945, or 1985.

"How long you had this ole truck, Gramps?"

"About a hundred and eleventy-seven years, boy, give or take leap year." He munched enjoyably on his own sandwich, looking down at his precious passenger with eyes of bright fun.

"That's a long while," Carlos observed, big eyes solemn. "Gramp. Gramp, is you really as old as my Daddy says?"

"Older," Old Pete said promptly, smiling. It didn't matter how old Orville claimed since neither of them had a clear notion about it. "I saw Crispus Attucks attack, and Moe Handus Gandhi sell candy. I remembers the bull fightin' at Bull Run." He scrubbed a wide, work-worn palm across the boy's softly-curled head. "I drove Henry's Ford, heard Franco bein' frank. I watched Napoleon nap, Hitler hit, and I saw ole Goering gore those *same* bulls."

"You ever seen Doctor King, Gramp?"

"Laws to make folks *civil!*" Pete paused, shook his head. "I don't have no real jokes 'bout him, child. None about Jesus, and none about Miz Latitude, neither." Seeing he was getting awful serious, the old man winked at the boy. "Don't you pay no mind to your old Gramp's silly stories, you hear? You're smart enough t' tell the difference. Just you believe Gramp when he's tellin' you *straight*, hear? All right?"

Carlos nodded soberly. It was quiet in the cab of the Memory Van for several moments. Carlos studied the old man's profile in a series of careful, sidelong glances, feeling awe. He wouldn't have dreamed of trying to read Gramp's thoughts, because they were so powerful they might sizzle a small boy's soul; but he knew the old man had brought him to Arby's for a reason, and he was richly complimented. Carlos' grandfather, he knew for a fact, was the wisest man in the whole world, and the oldest too. Anybody could tell that, for sure. Even Andy and Missy, down the street, so dumb they didn't know how to make pennies boogaloo or how to turn snowmen into running, cold rivulets that showed the spring hiding beneath the whiteness—*they'd* know how wise Gramp was, if they ever had the nerve and the sense to meet him, to listen to him. Right now, Carlos was willing to bet, Gramp was remembering Adam and Eve even. He'd *known* Noah, after all!

But Pete wasn't remembering the past; he was remembering the future, picturing that nice Mr. Doyle, the spirit, and how lonely he was, how desperate. Seeing some of the trouble that lay ahead for Carlos, and worse mischief in store for himself. It would be nice to have a talk with the boy and warn him against allowing the development of his farsight, and the funny little tricks he could do. Having special ways was only half a blessing, if that. But telling Carlos to stop was like asking the Mississippi to flow into a pot, please, and be boiled for coffee.

It was odd, the way grandpas got along better with their grandsons than their own children. Pete grinned behind his last bite of sandwich and the soggy, tasty paper it was in. Miz Latitude, who'd known more things of *real* nature than anybody Old Pete ever met, used to tell him it was because of the stars—the planet Neptune, to be exact. Old Neptune influenced people's beliefs, the way they wished things were, and how they pretended life actually was. She'd told Pete it took Neptune almost fourteen years to pass through a single sign of the zodiac, 'cause it was one of the distant or outer planets that took longest to do it. So if a man had his Neptune early in Cancer, when he was born, the chances were his own boy would have the planet in the *next* sign down the zodiac, and the two of them didn't have much in common. But years later, when the old man's grandson came along, *he'd* have the planet of dreams, illusions, belief and magic *two* signs away, and that was a sextile—sixty degrees. Which meant that an old grandpa and his grandson really had more in common, more to share, than a daddy and his boy.

Well, Pete reflected, wiping his lips with a napkin

and turning slowly on the seat, *leastways it* seems *that way 'tween Carlos and me.*

"Honey," he said aloud, "it's all right to be the way you are." He clasped his hand over the boy's. "No, it's better than that. It's fine. It is fine to know special things."

There was no immediate answer. Carlos was thinking; feeling. From his own standpoint there was no reason for suprise that Gramp knew about all the things he could do, since Gramp knew just about everything worth knowing. But he also sensed, with the old man's kindly gaze upon him, that his Gramp was telling him that his talents would continue to grow and that there might even be *more* of them. And that was one thing Carlos didn't want, at all.

"They make me so *different*," he cried. Suddenly raising his head, looking up at Gramp, his handsome young face was illumined by the headlights of a passing automobile. There were tears smarting in his eyes and he didn't want Gramp to think he was a sissy, so he tried winking them back. But they kept coming and, inside, he was seeing now the kids down the block —Missy and Andy, the white girl and boy who kept staring up the street at him as if they'd really like to play, but who also looked away when he called to them and remained near their own house. "Gramp, I'm too different *now!*"

Old Pete saw the same picture seen by his grandson, and sighed. "It's what the Lord wants for you, child. The way he makes some younguns tall, and fast as the wind. He wants you to be a carrier of the special knowing, Carlos." He patted the cracked back of the boy's seat. "He wants you to have a Memory Van of your own, honey, and take away all the hurt you can find."

"Our teacher said folks like us are witches, Gramp—evil." Carlos shuddered. "She said they used to *burn* people who can look ahead, who have dreams about things that aren't real."

"That's true. That's what happened. And maybe some folks with our talents do bad things with them, from time to time. People with different talents do evil with them, too, don't they?" Old Pete cupped the child's chin and looked into his shining eyes. "Who made us, Carlos?"

"God," the boy replied at once. "God made us."

"Did God ever make anything bad?" Pete paused to let it sink in. "Do you think He just made our heads, and our arms and legs? Didn't He make the talents we have when we arrive on earth?" He saw Carlos nod. "You don't s'pose He takes a break, wh en he's busy creatin', and the old devil sits in for Him t' add *bad* things?" He saw Carlos laugh. "There ain't nothin' wrong with different boy, long as it's good and don't hurt nobody." He hesitated, then concluded there was nothing wrong with what he wanted to do, either. Carefully, gently, he began introducing the thought-forms in his own mind to Carlos and made him see them clearly. "Martin Luther King was different. Ole Abraham Lincoln, *he* was different. George Washington Carver and Jackie Robinson, *they* were different too." He saw Carlos' eyes grow big with a realization of what his grandfather could do, steadily letting a series of images parade past the child's mind's eye.

He'd saved a special one for last and projected it with tenderness. "Jesus was also different, Carlos."

"But what *good* is the talent, Gramp?" He got to his knees on the truck seat in a motion of frustration and doubt. He seized the big hand nearest him, and held it against his heart. "Gramp, lots of those folks got themselves *killed!*"

Pete's fingers squeezed the little hand. The heartbeat was good, strong; a valiant heart. "Honey, look at me," he said. "I'm still here. I'm here to guide you, and protect you, and that's what a lot of people with our gifts didn't have. Somebody to teach 'em the ways. Who understood what I want to tell you now: God gave you the talent to *help people*, that's the answer, pure and simple. That's why He handed out most of the talents He did, whether folks build 'em into something fine or let 'em rot. You're here to *help*, 'cause that serves God, and Jesus, and all those other people you saw. Child, that's the only reason."

The boy's gaze locked with his and the strength of what the grandfather said, the sincerity of all that he meant, momentarily made them one. Carlos settled back into his seat, suddenly sleepy.

"Try not to upset your Daddy or your Momma with it," Pete added in an affectionate tone. "They're different, too, y'see. Differences work both ways."

"But what kind of talent do they have, Gramp?" Carlos asked quietly. He looked drowsily out the window, saw the lights go out in the restaurant. It would be much darker soon. "Do you know?"

Old Pete sighed and revved up the ancient motor of

the Memory Van. "God knows, child," he said, backing up, "what happens to half the gifts He gives folks. I reckon they just don't want them."

CHAPTER 13

I couldn't for the life of me (if that term isn't in such rotten taste it makes you gag) figure out what to do next. The situation was nearer to Completely Unacceptable than anything I could remember except Pop dying, and, years before that, an old mongrel heart-tugger I'd owned at the age of thirteen.

But while I was down on my knees before my own bedroom door anyway, where my own wife and my best friend had gone to get better acquainted—thereby making me wonder if anyone ever truly "owned" or held permanent title to anybody or anything—all that occurred to me was prayer.

I guess that's what a lot of us do, when we're finally convinced that nothing else is left. Which, now that I thought of it, would annoy the crap out of me, if I were in God's position. "Thanks awfully, but did you misplace the number?" Because it's lousy manners and not very practical, when you get down to it. Being the Court of Last Resort when you've told people, in writing, that they can move *mountains* if their faith is strong enough, is not exactly a compliment to the Creator. It's like telling your kid you'll always be willing to lend a helping hand, the door's open and the coffee's on, and then hearing they've sold dope to get out of a jam. Really, you'd feel terrible! "Don't call me, I'll call *you*," I'd inform the late-late prayer-maker who gets around to it after Johnny Carson. Then I would break the connection and murmur, "Sylvia dear, if that person calls back, find out if he wants to thank me for delaying him last week so he'd stay out of that six-car collision, or for the week before when he was scheduled to get cancer. Remember that one? I made it a cold, instead."

So I set out to pray for some kind of *alternate universe*, since there didn't seem to be much left for me in the line of options. You know, a world in which I was either decently dead and collected, or genuinely alive so I could paste Mike Abernethy in the mouth. Well, I'm not sure when it was that *you* prayed most recently but I'd been pretty casual about it. Most people, I thought, were either persuaded by their family allegiances to contact the Creator regularly, preferably over the weekend when there were others praying and you didn't feel so grovelly about it, or forgot about Him until ceremonies like weddings. And funerals. Which, again, would not make *me* a bundle of generosity; but nobody's nominated Zach Doyle for the job anyway, even though they could start entering my name for sainthood now, if they wanted to.

But I hadn't done anything more than nod my head, try to hang on to my screeching nerves and far more explosive temper, and fumble around for a few meaningfully respectful words, when two things happened simultaneously: I knew that I was so outraged, so filled with a sense of injustice, that what I was attempting was little more than a travesty of prayers; and, looking down at my feet, I saw this *aura* begin sweeping up my body!

It happens that I'd read a few paragraphs of a book which dealt with the question of auras, or haloes, and I remembered then what I'd learned: the artists who'd painted priceless works of art depicting Jesus and His Apostles with haloes had meant well but generally misunderstood a concept that went back to believers in the occult or supernatural. Always, it seemed, there'd been highly sensitive people who were capable of making out a shimmering light around others. Eastern occultists had claimed that this emanation, a light or aura, was actually the ethereal body of an individual —a luminous "outer coat" which might or might not contain the soul, or that similarly elusive article we call a human mind. It existed around or "clothed," they'd said, all living things. And now, over the past several years, the developments of a scientific method known as Kirlian photography seemed to have entirely validated those beliefs which went back many centuries in time. Because, with that photographic process, using no hand-holding seances, mediums or even incense, it was possible not only to take pictures of the vividly-brilliant aura, but establish a wonderful fact: when a finger was severed from a hand, or a portion of a leaf broken away, the aura of the missing portion *still photographed!*

As if it still *was there*, hauntingly, in the fashion of a ghost separated from its original body.

I'd read many other things, too, but they always seemed not to "impact" me directly and besides, my memory used to be the most fallible thing about me. I recall telling people it was sensible to keep the old brain sparsely furnished, to permit incoming flashes of genuis; that one could always look things up. I'd read that psychics sometimes could detect the mental state and physical well-being of another person by perceiving the *color* of the halo, or aura.

I definitely do not remember what the different colors signified. Mine, I saw, was nearly colorless, at first. Then as it climbed my frame into visibility, it became a pale and twinkling pink—and finally, blanketing me from head to foot, a near-blinding, blazing scarlet.

And that, I think, is when I'd had enough and started doing crazy things.

There was no way my Louise would go to bed with Mike Abernethy if she was aware that my consciousness existed, and that I knew what she was doing. There was also no way Mike would have suggested it, because, after I'd discovered my ability to probe deeply into the way my sweet pal actually felt about women, I'd found at once that his kind is chicken through and through. Not that I hoped to make Louise realize I'd survived. I just wanted to stop Michael Abernethy from using her, and me, the way he had everybody else he'd known in their vulnerable misery.

Rising from my kneeling posture, my prayer incomplete yet possibly answered, I knew further that I'd been right in believing I had latent powers of compensation finally stirring within me. I knew it, then; I had no doubt; and I *did* it.

First, I called for thunder.

It came rumbling across the night plain of low winter's sky like a herd of phantom buffalo. It was furious and mindlessly vindictive, the way I'd wanted it. It made the floorboards rock 'n roll and all the windows in the house shake with psychic St. Vitus. The panes would tumble out, shattering noisily, if I asked. Instead, I made a director's "cut" gesture, then raised my hand, pointed my index finger at the heavens and brought it *down*, sharply—in the direction of the bedroom.

Violent lightning snapped and crackled outside the windows in there and I could tell the way it lit up the entire room by its sensationally sizzling dance along the gap under the door. It went on thundering, too, booming like all the basso voices of a chorus of angry gods, until a male voice, the newly-shaky one belonging to my old friend Mike, demanded, *"What the hell?"*

I gave him an answer. Seeing the picture clear in my mind, I caused unseen fists to pound like pixilated poltergeists on all the walls in the bedroom. I made invisible Dickensian chains drag clankingly across the floor. The noises were all but deafening, and I found myself jumping up and down in mischievous delight. Somehow I'd managed to give an echo chamber effect to the clattering chains that would have done an ace sound man credit. *OOoooooo!* I crooned my vengeance joyfully, and my rapturous revenge rippled from the windows and ceiling of the bedroom, like the old Ink Spots had died and gone mad and clung from the curtains and fixtures—*OoOO-oo-oo, OoOO-oo-oo!*

That accidental effect gave me an idea so I threw back my head and started laughing weirdly, crazily, and the sound postively *boomed* inside my old bedroom, the fear-inspiring, manic cackling of a madman who'd permeated the walls, the windows, the closet and the ceiling and the floorboards. I admit it, it was just fantastic! I *liked* it, I really grooved on it like some sixteen-year-old smartass going out of his tree on uppers. I'll also confess the possibility that maybe I didn't have to *pretend* to sound like a lunatic, but let that go, forget that, because I dug it so damned much I did it *again,* and put more feeling into it!

Two living bodies in that room, scrambling to sit up, to make it stop. I heard and identified those noises at once, because I'd *intended* just such a reaction—I had meant to *pray* for this!

For a moment I stood outside that door I'd passed through ten thousand times, generally yawning and sleepy but sometimes romantic or horny; and my fists were doubled and I had this smile on my face and I guess I was psychotically happy as Hitler when they told him France was his. Even then, I like to think, there was some deepdown part of me that was trying to get my attention, muttering, "*Hold* it, Zach, whoa, baby, this isn't precisely what we call *human*," but I didn't pay any attention.

If Mike Abernethy was going to make it with Zachary Edson Doyle's beloved and beautiful widow, he was going to need the nervous system to the people singing hymns on the Titanic!

I did variations, for another moment or two, giggling way high up off the roof of my mouth, tossing in a juicy gurgle, and listened to the two of them thrashing around. Then I focused my gaze on the door to the bedroom, getting the whole vertical chunk of wood just so in my mind, tensed, and *zapped* the door with all my newly-found might!

It flew open, banging off the wall! Except that doesn't do it justice. It postively *exploded* into the room, splintering down the middle as it collided with the wall, then sort of weakly dangling, vibrating, by a single hinge.

Louise still had some of her clothes on and was leaning back against the headboard, both hands over her mouth. Abernethy was a terrified scarecrow balanced on one skinny leg, trying to get his pants on. Man, my heart *exulted!* He looked out of his gourd with terror. Myopically, because his glasses were still on the nightstand—*my* nightstand, on *my* side of the bed—Mike was looking around, blinking a hundred miles per hour as he strove to see the source of his terror.

I squeezed my lids shut, and concentrated. His hornrimmed specs rose from the stand, hovered for a second, then flew at his face and hooked themselves behind his ears. I'll never forget the sound he made, then; a piggy kind of squeal, which was followed by a

145

mad dash for the open door. He had one shoe on, no socks, and he looked a lot more pale than I imagined myself to look as I stepped aside and let him go. Not once did he glance back at Louise, or even call her name; *not once!* That's my justification, I guess.

Because when he'd gone and I turned to look at her, I saw immediately that she was perilously close to a fullfledged heart attack.

That had never been my intention, certainly not consciously. Horrified, I ran to her and tried to take her hand, to caress her forehead. I was so concerned for her that I must have given off some sort of discernible coldness; because she suddenly shrank back against the headboard, scarcely able to breathe, her knees pulled up to her chin. She looked like a little girl to me—a little girl who was close to death. I'd forgotten about her heart condition, entirely forgotten it in my anxiety to stop them and (can I *say* it?) get even. Never in my entire existence had I caused fear to show upon her lovely features or wanted it to be there. I swear, I'd never wanted to see my girl afraid of me!

Careful not to get too close again and create the shiver of fear that seemed to be all I could ever bring her now, I whispered tenderly and softly to her, hoping to calm her and restore her health. I tried with all my new-found power to project to Louise a picture of the many good times we'd shared, the handful of celebrating moments and the special times of silliness and even the sad times that were at least ours together. I did everything I could think of to assure her that I'd loved her, cursing the fact that, like many people, I'd never said it enough, never *showed* it enough. I told her I would always love her, that I longed for the time when she'd come to me but that I'd never, ever try to *make* it happen; and slowly, very slowly, the color began to come back into her soft cheeks and she regained the power to breathe naturally.

Oh, how I wanted to kiss her one last time.

But I stood, moving away from the bed, knowing finally that she'd been right to put her life back together the best she could, knowing that life, in truth, was for the living and did not include me.

I went out into the hall, then jogged soundlessly downstairs and out to the front yard. I heard a muffled bark, saw a low-hung shadow bulk and move. Angelo wanted to go with me, I think. He approached me in that goofily indirect, vague manner with which he'd found me again. But I used my thoughts to open the door and gently urge him back into the house, for the simple reason that even a house pet, a clumpy old dog, has the right to its life. It wasn't only that obvious thing that we all say, that people killed too much; it was how we *let* creatures die, thoughtlessly, without lifting a finger to help. It was how we seemed incapable of understanding that death wasn't an explosive event every time; it could be a process, one we sometimes were able to reverse by caring.

The night was clear, unfazed by my apparitional hijinks. It had been illusion. Here and there, I saw, snow had melted, perhaps there'd be no more that winter. It lay in the future, but spring surely had to come at last and they called that a period of rebirth. Possibly I might hope *my* time coincided with it; perhaps I'd simply come to consciousness in my grave too soon, or somehow died too early. Everything was a screwed-up mess, these days; maybe even heaven and hell didn't quite know what was coming down—or meant to go *up*.

I looked toward the second story of the structure I'd idly called "home," my place; and I'm not really sure whether I drew Louise to the window or not. But she came anyway, as if looking for me. She'd always been there for me. I knew that, at least; and as she was frozen in the window frame I realized there was more puzzledness in her face than fear. That was good. She'd be all right, I thought. Mike would not dare return after the ludicrous display he'd made of himself. As for her other man, well, he was going to leave her alone forever. Which is why I did everything I could to sort of photograph her features with my uplifted eyes, striving with intense yearning to memorize everything about my girl, my wife. My widow.

When at last she closed the drapes, I turned to look through tears at my familiar street. A kid in an old junker clunked by, oblivious to me. Across the way, my neighbors Mary and Jerry still had their Christmas tree up and I smiled, nodding. They loved it, they hated to take it down. And when they did, sometimes not until February, it was only the unavoidable reminder that all seasons and all things draw to an end.

But why couldn't I? And where would I *go?*

CHAPTER 14

"Honesty compels me to confess quite readily, Link," Wells growled from his side of the polished desk, "that you have succeeded in rendering me speechless." He lowered his great head sadly so that it rested upon his infinity of chin-folds. The effect was that of a collapsed accordion with beseeching eyes peering up at his standing, fastidiously dressed host. "Virtually *speechless*," added the angel, as if the achievement of his opposite number was both baffling and a stupendous triumph.

"As the expression goes—kindly do not read more into it than simple colloquialism, old chap—'thank God for small mercies.' Although," Newton Link added, his mortician-trimmed mustache twitching above a noticeable smirk, "I dare say most souls of your acquaintance might quibble about the adjectival 'small.'

149

A large, cumbersomely well-meaning one perhaps. And I *do* wish you'd stop 'confessing' things to me, especially from that heartfelt 'honesty' of yours." Link's tailored shoulders shrugged with minor irritation. "A question of taste, and suitability; you can see that."

"For decade after decade, for century upon spent century, we have been thrown together in our perpetual quest for mutual understanding. On the behalf of a greater good, or call it greater *objective*, if you desire." Chauncey Wells' well-padded buttocks sank measurably lower into the stiff-backed chair offered to him this time. He looked rather like a composite of Orson Welles and an overly indulgent Sir Winston Churchill and was entirely aware of it. He'd even looked in once on the latter, upon his arrival, and consciously memorized the Briton's mannerisms. "Thrown together for the propagation, nay, the ultimate survival of our grave and fundamental firms." Wells sighed. "There was a time when I genuinely believed I had come to know you well. Innocent fool, I."

"Your choice of expression, old man," Link said shortly. He'd fallen to work at his desk, certain there was a point to the angel's oratory. "You've lost nothing at all over the time-span. I really must guard myself against your, ah, unctuous suasion. You should write an autobiography entitled 'Mr. Blandishment Builds His Dream Heaven,' or possibly, '101 Ways to Bore Your Enemy Into Submission.' "

"Your perfidy, sir, is beyond comprehension." Only

Wells' buttery, pursed lips moved as he declaimed, and tapped a cane on the floor. "It doth not scale new heights but plungeth to fresh depths."

"Come, you'll turn my head!" Link, smiling, began adjusting dials on his precious computer. Now and then, shards of colored light leapt into the air; it was as if Newton were ruthlessly decimating a rainbow. "Do get to the point."

"I have arrived there," Wells rumbled, frowning. "You sir, are the most fully untrustworthy and deceitful, unremorsefully immoral individual I have encountered. I have no blood and sweat left, but I've found a reservoir of tears."

Link turned with a continental bow. "Thank you, thank you, and *again*, I thank you!" Then he pushed a black button with a manicured index finger and a picture swam quickly into milky focus on his viewscreen. He folded his arms then, to appraise the obese angel with his cold eyes. A mortal might have flinched. "Either you are deceiving me, you old psalm-singer, or you've become senile at last. Really, you've given me much to do if I am to set right your most recent aberration."

"Are you asking me seriously to believe that you are not at the source of Zachary Doyle's present plight—his apparent homelessness?" Wells' eyes widened in disbelief. "Do you really expect me to accept that nonsensical notion you had during our previous conference—that a *third party*, a viable new Organization, is coming into being after all this time?"

"Third parties are starting up incessantly on earth,"

Link retorted, his dark eyes snapping. "Not to mention some of the planets located in the northeast quadrant of the Sagonia star systems."

"What are you implying?" Chauncey leaned foward, eyes narrowing. He seemed pale, or more translucent—nearly frightened. "Rather, what are you *not* saying about those upstart liberals?"

"Well, it's nothing you won't be hearing soon enough anyway." Link shrugged, took his time about sitting upon the edge of his desk. "Now, I am not one to pass rumors along, old fellow, whatever else you may believe about me. But you're certainly aware of how unhappy some of the more free-thinking souls from other galaxies have become over the centuries? They have a deep, troubling feeling that your side still regards them as second-class citizens."

"Newton, things have always been that way," Wells said, trying to brush if off. "It's no doubt debatable from a sheerly liberatarian viewpoint, and it may sometimes seem authoritarian. But my Chief began the entire operation with earth, don't forget. The globe is home to Him, His baby, even if the press of other matters prevents Him from putting in appearances as often as He used to. All the little extras, the frills and polishes given to beings in other parts of the universe, were tried out first on earth."

"I've been told," Link said slowly, eyes boring into Wells', "that some of the beings you appear to consider mere afterthoughts see themselves as refinements, vastly superior to the original design."

Wells scowled. "They feel that way only because of the constant flow of propaganda from your side,

Newton—don't deny it. These newly emerging lifeforms may have a greater *capacity* for learning, but they're little more than savages. Giving advanced philosophical insights and a closer approximation of reality to member bodies of the Third World is like giving candy to an infant human, or glossalium to a tri-head." Chauncey pointed at Link. "It's as inexcusable as sending an agent to earth and confiding the basic formulae for atomic energy."

"Oh, that," Link said with a smile. "I'm trying to discuss the *cosmos* with you, Wells! A bit less narrowness, please."

"I *am* discussing the bigger, broader picture," Chauncey argued. "Look, Newton: with the passage of time, with a little patience, the newer chaps will be entitled to the identical rights as the rest of the colonists, but they must *earn* it, it doesn't happen over an epoch! You know that's been the stand of my Organization for millions of millenia. Just because *your* Chief tries to subvert tradition by sending out a delegation of Redshirts with suitcases filled with new aphorisms and expedient moral exceptions, blowing smoke and full of hot air, doesn't alter the time-honored precepts for evolutionary evaluation or quantum-jump quintessene!"

"You won't believe me," Link asked, "when I tell you some of the tri-heads and compucreatures are getting organized? That they want someone new as Governor?"

Chauncey Wells relaxed. It had been another smokescreen, as he thought. "Do you," he asked softly, "take me for a fool?"

"That, my dear old cherubic chum, is one of the temptations we bypass." He smiled, seeming not at all upset by being caught redhanded again at the ancient game. "Forever, it has been your side which persists in underestimating the opposition, Wells. Evil, you see, takes nothing for granted. We have a saying: 'Drop a detail, delight a deity.' And that is precisely the reasoning behind the way our representatives on earth and the other planets with life have sometimes appeared to be gratuitously violent, or ruthless—disposed to 'lay waste,' to borrow your own melodramatic phrasing."

"I don't follow you," Wells confessed.

"Alas, you never have," Link sighed. "I am saying that it is *good* which sees its foe's movements as silly or trendy, as error-prone and certain to be quickly vanquished. I always instruct the newcomers to my department to assume there is a rational purpose behind your side's penchant for sentimental whims, emotional allowances. For forbearance, for the taking of ludicrous chances—for example, with the very laws you support. My aides, while they are universally demon workers, find it difficult to believe they lost their lives and souls in the face of such overblown grandness."

"Sticks and stones, Newton." Stiffly, Wells stood. By now, he was fairly sure his ephemeral apparatus was all but permanently marred by the wicked weather, by trying to rest in chambers with punk rock music suffusing the corridors, and being obliged to dine in restaurants which featured not only the most fattening foods in the universe but the most tempting and total beverage list he'd ever seen. He longed to liberate the spirit of Zachary Doyle and now, for the first time, he thought he saw the end in sight. But it would not do to let Link know as much. "It was against the joint policy statement of 1641 and the contractual amendments of 1802 to allow Doyle to use celestial sorcery."

"I know," Link said with a gesture. "It's clearly stated, witnessed, and signed twice in blood that only certified and long-term spectral agents are entitled to engage in such dangerous avocational pastimes."

"And *then*," Wells amended, leaning on the desk, "only by the specific terms implied by your supernal signature and mine! Link, that fellow was virtually out of control! Do you know that he exhausted nearly thirty cloisters of effervescence, six oblations of soluble saturation, and an unconcentrated kilo of fervid sirocco?" His chins trembled. "Why, the Archangel's anemometer went right off the *wall!*"

Link seemed pained. "I felt badly about Doyle. His best friend bedding his widow and no recourse left to him. It wasn't out of character for me to weaken or, for that matter, to permit him a show of violence." He offered a hand, and his smile. "Wells, it won't happen again."

Chauncey was surprised. Newton Link looked contrite! It was true that the rascal had seen more of Wells than ever before and Records contained a number of yellowing parchments, reporting after-death conversions. Besides, unsaid by both of them was the fact that they'd lost a great deal of control of the wandering spirit. Away from his own house, what could conceivably lure Zach Doyle either to the basement or to his cleaned-out cubbyhole? Now, at last, it might be possible to work with Link, even to bag one of the all-time biggies. He took the proferred hand tenderly, ignoring the steam rising from between their palms. "My very good fellow," he said simply.

Link refrained from wincing until his obese counterpart had left. Then, just to remind himself, he metamorphosed into his actual appearance and preened for some ameliorating moments before a full-length mirror. It was no wonder his secretarial ogress had swooned, then been taken over to Psychology for second-degree shock. His glory was in horror, in the image he saved for just the ideal moments, and Ms. Moloch would be in the very best of claws, since Psych was better staffed than any other professional department in the lower level.

Wells, Link reflected with pleasure, might literally be succumbing finally to senility, just as he had maliciously joked.

Because there was certainly no reason now for the dejected spirit of Zachary Edson Doyle to visit his silly writer's aerie in the garage; but the fellow would be furnished with ample reason to come back to his *basement* and to make the symbolic decent into the seething world which Newton Link privately considered his *Baaliwick*.

Returning to his dignified disguise, since even his Chief and the members of the corporate counsel couldn't bear looking at his genuine magnificence, Link turned to his computer viewscreen.

It was her fortune that Louise Doyle could not see the perfectly loathesome smile of lust beaming at her from another dimension of sight, sound, and sanity.

CHAPTER 15

He'd gone out front to play, bundled up by Daddy so envelopingly that he seemed more to roll down the lane than to walk. Another time, he might have giggled that fine, healthy, life-loving giggle of his; but not today. Once he'd reached the sidewalk he didn't know what to do. The snow he hadn't idly melted away himself was turning now to lifeless, boring slush and there was no way he could build a snowman, or even make respectable snowballs, from what remained. It was a minor and impersonal loss and the boy sensed it should not upset him, but it did. He discovered he was starting to cry and clenched his fists in his brightly-colored mittens, looking off down the street where the other children lived, the ones who were just a little boy and a little girl like kids everywhere. The wind was cold. It bit the boy's nose and he blamed it for his tears.

He felt so strange. Today there was a bewilderment in his mind and in his heart that lurked like some avid monster in a comic book, or maybe more like a ferocious tiger on TV that had been shot by one of those tranquilizer guns. And if he caused the tingling lump of dullness edging his confusion to disappear, if he let that old beast up, he knew it would devour him. Since he wouldn't be ten years old for awhile yet—ten was the big age, it came with *two* numbers and he had longed to be TEN so long it felt like forever—he couldn't have put any of his feelings into words.

But he felt that people were asking him not to be Carlos anymore. To become something different. Something that was really more like them, like his teachers and the white kids down the block and like Momma and everybody who couldn't do the things his Gramp and he could do.

Carlos had been to see the shrink.

That was yesterday. This morning Carlos had arisen from bed and stood before the mirror, then in front of lots of things around the house, trying to see if he was any smaller yet. At first, the answer had seemed to be No. Both Daddy and Gramp looked like giants still but not any more gigantic than before visiting Doctor Sapers. Carlos had tried on every shirt and pair of pants he owned and they'd all fitted, or not quite fitted, just the way they'd been the day before.

Now, however, blinking back tears as he stared down the street, the boy saw that he'd been wrong, and nodded his head. The shrink was making him smaller, all right. But it was happening *inside*, where nobody could see.

Nobody but Carlos himself.

He'd watched that old doctor-man real close while he asked dumb questions and scribbled in a book of pages with lines, and he'd listened, too. Maybe it was bragging but Carlos believed he knew more at the end of his fifty minutes about old Doctor Sapers than the shrink knew about Carlos! Like the way that doctor thought it was funny for a black lady to bring in her boy at rates like his, and didn't believe Momma was a model at all. He thought she was something starting with "pos" or "pros." Which just showed what *he* knew! He'd pretended to listen to what Momma had to say about Carlos' "little tricks" and muttered the word "psychokinesis" even while a part of his mind curled up in a sneer. That was when Carlos realized Doctor Sapers had only one belief in his name, mainly a belief in that thing called Psychiatry, which was what made him think he was so smart. And that was a terrible shame, since there were so many other *fine* things to believe in. Carlos had tried his best to feel sorry for the shrink. With Momma waiting outside, smiling and looking beautiful but tapping her foot and feeling terribly ashamed of him, Carlos had listened intently to all the words Doctor Sapers spoke. And gradually, he'd realized that the man was very smart, that he might know almost as much as Gramp if he didn't hate so many things and folks as he did. And Carlos had nodded at the right places, even worked hard at believing the same things Doctor Sapers believed about the "Psych" word. Because it made a lot of sense, now and then; parts of it explained a batch of stuff, even though other things were so silly they made Carlos want to laugh out loud.

Until it began to dawn on Carlos that the main thing this white man was saying to him was that he, Carlos, was *wrong*. Not mistaken, like on tests at school; *wrong*. Everything about him, from head to toe, inside as well as outside—and also that he was *sick*. The picture in Doctor Sapers' mind came into Carlos' head without effort and it made the boy feel like screaming, or throwing up. Because the picture this man almost-as-smart-as-Gramp had of him concerned the awful, sick things messing around in his head like wild animals that had to come out.

All the things Carlos had believed were his very *best* parts. Which probably showed just how . . . sick . . . he was.

Andy and Missy came out of their house, strode right down to the sidewalk, and turned to walk toward him. Carlos saw them coming but he was so lost in his own thoughts, suddenly finding that his shame was beginning to turn to anger, that he didn't realize what was happening until the little white boy and girl were only a few feet away. Then he understood that he had called them, somehow, beckoned to them to come play. And they had, they'd hurried out of their house and were waiting, now, for him to say what he wanted.

Carlos grinned. What he wanted was friends. What he wanted was to play, to have a nice time. And instead of saying anything, he *showed* them what he wanted, with the only toys that meant anything to him.

"He's doin' it again," Orville said into the phone. He'd pulled back the drapes all the way so he could see the three children from inside the dining room, and then kept his promise to Alma Jo, hating every minute of it. "He's got those honky brats from down the street positively *hypnotized* with his magic tricks." Despite himself, Orville smiled. Alma Jo couldn't see it. "Man, he's somethin' else!"

"Public institutions are full of people who are 'something else,' Orville." Her voice in his ear from the telephone receiver wasn't the soft, almost crooning one he used to hear from the pillow beside his. It wasn't even the amused, sarcastic one that spoke of how her figure was what fed all of them, "even that Tom you call a father." She didn't even go on to say that they'd never have been able to move into such a nice, clean, crime-free neighborhood if they'd had to depend upon Old Pete and Orville; she didn't even laugh and tell him that he and his father were the *white* sheep in her family. Alma Jo sounded fed up, and frightened. "Doctor Sapers said it's a classic case, possibly schizophrenia."

"If that boy's personality is split, baby," Orville said tightly, "it's split between you and me." She hadn't told him much that happened at the shrink's office. Now he wished he didn't have to hear it. "What else did your high-priced, high-powered mind-bender have to say about our boy?"

She didn't answer immediately and for a moment he thought she'd hung up. "Orv, the situation is worse than I'd imagined. Doctor Sapers may not be able to provide Carlos with adequate treatment on a once-a-week basis at his office."

Orville's finger clutched the phone harder. "Don't go on, Alma Jo." He was nearly begging. "Don't say the rest of it."

"Damn you, man, this is the *real world* out here!" She didn't raise her voice but the intensity of her frenzied whispers made his ears ring, and some of her careful, cultivated mannerisms melted like Carlos' snowman. "All you and that old man upstairs know is collectin' junk, sortin' through white folks' cast-offs in the—the *fantasy* that you'll stumble across Aladdin's lamp, or—or a goddamned *treasure* map! You won't even *try* to live in modern times, to blend in a little, and I can't even *tell* you what I've put up with to get as far as I have. If I did, sugar, you'd probably bust somebody's *head!*"

Orville nodded, shutting his eyes. Alma Jo had paused, catching her breath, waiting for him to ask her what she meant, to demand to know the name of the man, or men, who'd helped her get ahead. But Orville had guessed that much already. Alma Jo had the beauty, and the talent; she deserved what she had now, but that didn't have anything to do with it. And she talked to *him* about fantasy!

"Listen to me, Orville," she said, almost crying. "I am not going to let my success be taken away from me now. I'm not. Honey, I just *can't!*"

"Right; I get it." He nodded. In a nearly drowsy,

offhanded way, his gaze swept through the house, over the assortment of things he and Old Pete had brought home and the array of shiny, plastic things Alma Jo had bought. Outside, he saw, his son was actually entertaining little Missy and Andy; they were laughing, even applauding. He was proud of Carlos' conquests, glad his son was making friends at last.

But he also saw himself, twenty years earlier, and remembered how he had forced himself to turn against his own father's gifts. Because he'd seen the mind-reading, the knack for moving things with the power of the mind, all the magic which had given Old Pete dignity and self-worth, as nothing more than a psychic shoe-shine stand. As one more way, like boxing, basketball, singing or tapdancing, to sell oneself to a white audience by being genuinely superior but hiding it behind the toothy grins of the professional black in modern America.

He couldn't do any of those tricks any longer. There was no magic left in Orville. He'd given it all up because a pretty girl had lulled him with the whispers of a more modern series of illusions; and now it was too late to be either what she wanted or what he'd been meant to be. The only option remaining to him was a worse stereotype: the useless, rootless black dude of a dad who cut loose and ran.

That was the one change Orville couldn't accommodate. "You're sayin' we may have to put Carlos away. Get his head fixed, trimmed down to size so it fits into that real world you mentioned." He heard her start to protest, to describe it in other words, and laughed. "Whoa, lover, Orville didn't say no! Orville don't *ever* say no, you know that! We'll do whatever your white doctor thinks best. But don't *prettify* it, right? Don't ask me to *believe* in your magic, or his. Just tell me what you want!"

Then he hung up, not even slamming the phone down, standing awhile to watch his son at play, realizing that his main mistake had been in failing to see that everybody, black or white, ran a shoe-shine stand if he wanted to survive in the world. Everybody bucked-and-winged, flashed all the gleaming white teeth in his head, sang his heart out, and hoped people'd throw enough nickels and dimes to keep him from starving.

But the trouble with it, from their viewpoint, was plain to see when you watched Missy giggle and little Andy spontaneously hug his newfound friend: *this* was what Carlos had going for him.

Carlos wasn't ever going to be seven feet tall with a great hookshot.

Old Pete, too, had been enjoying the scene from his bedroom window on the second floor, glad that his grandson was having a good time and making friends. Hopeful, too, that what Miz Latitude had said was wrong, even if she'd never missed one prophecy in life, and it didn't make sense to think dying had hurt her special gifts.

The old man smiled with pride. The kids below were just talking now, getting acquainted, asking who you are and saying who I am, the way folks had done since the good Lord made folks. They'd put aside Carlos' magic for the time being, and that was fine, good and proper. There was nothing wrong with being ordinary, normal, common. What *was* wrong, Old Pete believed, was reaching out too fast to embrace the commonplace, so fast a person forgot to check himself out to see if he or she had anything *special* that might make this old world a better place. Or a more interesting one.

It was fine, what Carlos was doing; his Gramp approved, until the old man's mind gently probed, tried to touch the unique mind of his beloved grandson—

And found that Carlos was blocking it from him. Keeping him out.

It had to be that way, since the boy knew Pete was the only one around who could reach inside. But the experience was entirely new to the old man; Carlos had never hidden his thoughts from his Gramp.

The boy's huge, serious, mesmeric eyes were on his immediately when Old Pete looked through the window again, as if he had *expected* him to try to make contact. Carlos' powers were growing, there was no question about that. They were growing more impressive every week and they would probably be stronger than his Gramp's one fine day.

But why was he suddenly keeping secrets? What did he mean to *do* with his gift from God?

When Carlos broke the gaze, looked away, Old Pete caught a quick peek inside. Nobody else in the world could have seen it that fast now that Miz Latitude was gone. *Ain't going to shrink me*, that was the thought in the boy's mind. And more, fading out of view even as the old man snatched the words and tucked them into his own extraordinary head: *I won't let 'em*.

The old man sat down in his rocker, one of the few pieces of furniture he'd ever bought himself. He leaned back to get it going, one big toe occasionally prodding gently against the floor.

When he felt Carlos' own thoughts almost shyly, guiltily tapping at the door to his mind, Pete brushed them aside. He did't want apologies. He wanted to know how his grandson planned to stop so many adults from doing what they pleased with him.

CHAPTER 16

King of all I surveyed—monarch, ultimate ruler, *emperor of everything!*

With my arms outthrust in a gesture of generosity, I looked about me in all directions, beaming benignly and sharing my colossal glory with all that which met my all-knowing eye. Mine was a heady existence, an extraordinary one. No, no; more than that, I realized quickly (being the only one who could correct my majestic grandness); *much* more. Mine was a *unique* existence, and I, Zachary Edson Doyle, was the most unique being in the whole universe!

My welcoming arms dropped and my chin sagged. I saw the depressing age of my universe, my world, and the way life busily builds layers of cobwebs and dust over everything that stops moving. That was as far as I ever got with that particular attempt at madness, or say rather, the attempt to *adjust* to madness. Even though I had been a writer once in some implausibly distant time—one hundred million minutes ago, perhaps, or longer—and so I kept blundering into the same language trap, instance after instance: the word "unique" means one of a kind. It has exclusivity to it. I had learned, one hundred and *ten* million minutes ago or so, that it was impossible to have *degrees* of uniqueness. One either was, or wasn't, unique. Just as there actually could not be a plural "eternity."

So it was that the harder I strove to adjust to going mad, my own educational experience and knowledge kept hurling me back, as if I'd rebounded from an unseen forcefield. It was, I'd recently concluded during another of my full-voiced, regal, pompous tirades, some kind of unasked-for failsafe method that living, human logic had programmed into my memory cells and, so long as I had my memory, I would not be permitted the luxury of madness. Or even of becoming more unique than anyone, or anything, else.

Why was it that there were impenetrable, unviolable laws—absolutes—about the English language and not for people?

But that did take care of another day. Planning and acting out my little lunatic's playlet had eaten up the morning and nibbled a chunk out of afternoon while I tromped around the abandoned house which I tried to see as my imperial palace and beamed (as noted) upon my subjects: A mammoth chifferobe and a sheetless bed in one of the upstairs bedrooms; the massing of still disturbing shadows at the end of the long, dark corridor of the second story; the nonfunctioning and mostly shattered crystal chandelier in the ample dining room (which I sometimes sent swinging, to and fro, merely to watch an imitation of life's motion); a card-table plus two rickety chairs in the rec room, and a broken pool cue; a grandfather's clock which existed in the terminal stages of self-bemused senility, telling unbelievable lies about the time; a three-legged sofa in the massive living room; and the family of mice which shared the interior of the kitchen well with a fat and cunning spider. The mice did not seem to notice the spider, or vice versa; the spider and family of mice did not seem to notice *me*. I'd also found, in two or three closets, dresses and shirts and pants on hangers which I was saving for the time when I so desperately needed to see people that I would attempt to get them all jitterbugging around on the dank wood floors at the same time.

The mice and the spider, the clothing and the articles of furniture profligately left behind, were my royal subjects when I wished to amuse myself with madness. They were also my last possessions when wishing would no longer make it so, even for an evening.

It seemed odd to me that I cannot recall, during the whole period of my adult life, any sense of urgency or panic about having nothing to do. Quite the contrary. Like most people, I'd generally felt that I was always on the go, under pressure, constantly busy. I had yearned for spare, leisure, or "free time" when I could do whatever I wished to do. The couple of vacations Louise, the boys and I had taken I had looked forward to with the joyous anticipation we Christians should have for heaven itself, even if they weren't as enjoyable as any of us had expected. I'd never seemed to have enough time to do all the things I thought I wanted to do.

Now, each day yawned chasm-like before me, even though I'd managed to teach myself to lie down on the unmade second-floor bed and sleep—or "go away"—every night. At least, I believed it was night when I went upstairs; it was always dark in the house at those lonely moments and I may have confused inclement weather with bedtime on occasion.

I knew that I had come to this old barn of a house in the past. That much I could be sure of, since I wasn't in the process of moving in and I was reasonably certain that I'd been there longer than a day or two. Possibly longer than a week. Possibly, since they invented time—whoever or whatever had devised such a bizarre, limiting, and demanding thing. It was hard to tell. Because I continued to have this *concept* of a record-keeper, somewhere; of seconds, minutes, hours and days, but with no consistent points of reference. Oh, I planned eventually to squat crosslegged on the cold floor in the large kitchen and let the family of mice do it for me. Tell time, that is. (Another funny expression, that; "tell time." As if each of us had his own built-in Aesop, a rather simpleminded chap who cleared his throat as he arose, set the scene, and "told" us the story of Time. Which was, of course, a serial.) I had a notion that the mice came out to hunt for food at intervals which, since hunger happens to be a powerful motivator as well as an implacable enemy, would enable me to do something special (unique?):

invent a brand-new kind of time, give increments of it new names, make allowances for mousely ventures when Mom took longer than usual to sniff the air, or Junior was taken by an attack of stupidity and stumbled over his own feet. I figured a timing system devised by the rodents and me would be as workable and reasonable as any of the more established ones.

I yawned. I'm rather proud of that, and the stretching I do. They were artificial gestures, earlier, since I don't really get sleepy—or hungry, or sexy, or most of the things that cause living people so much trouble but also define the species to some extent. The yawn is to establish the fact that I will not let myself be overwhelmed by existing in this old pit of a place, that I'm "above" all that. The huge stretch I make is to reassure myself that I am relaxed, at ease now, unburdened by the interminable periods of actual Time which frighten me these days as much as dying or death used to concern me.

Because, you see, I have given up all hope of ever being "collected," of anybody smiling sympathetically and putting out a hand to lead me into the light, into a realm where explanations will be offered, and where other souls will speak with me and hug me and—

More yawns; more stretches. *I had to stop doing that!* I could not allow myself the luxury of self-pity, or of craving another, better afterlife. The pain and anguish of it had become acute, exquisite beyond anything I'd ever experienced as a living person. I could not afford to be self-destructive, since there was nothing left of myself to destruct. Except, of course, my mind; and that, as I already worked out (didn't I?)

could not occur until my memory was fully expunged.

This, surely, was what Catholics meant when they spoke of Purgatory.

Why the house was deserted, I did not know. To be honest about it, I'm not even sure exactly where it is. After looking a last time into Louise's eyes, when she came to the window that dreadful night, I had simply walked away, paying no attention whatsoever to the direction in which I was headed, or to how much time elapsed, if any, before I found this old house. It was, of course, a horror; I'd realized that, the minute I saw it. More than one hundred years old, filthy and rundown, apparently unoccupied for a decade or more, it sits back from the street on a sloping hill. Now, since the house has settled, it's at a crazy kind of angle and gives even me the notion when I glance nervously around the shadowed rooms of being just slightly *out of focus:* As if it existed in a parallel world only fractionally different from ours, but a world with different algebra and geometry, with swiftly-angled planes that suit alien eyes but seem forever weird, off-center, to me.

I'd wanted to be entirely alone after leaving my own house. Perhaps it was even providential that I'd found this place, and perhaps it did not even exist in the kind of reality I'd known. Maybe someone Unseeable had *willed* its existence, for me. Since I could be nothing but a nuisance for my widow, at best a reminder of days and nights that were as unreachable for Louise as they were for me, I'd come to the conclusion that we'd both be more contented if I left. But I had not wanted the company of strangers; oh, no. They certainly would not have known I was present, either. But their intimate conversations, their activity and commitments, would have been too hard to take—then and now, at least. Maybe in a century or two, I had reflected, I'd have my emotions under control enough to live, or exist, with people again, even assume a detached position in which I took vicarious delight in their doings. Once that was achieved, I could let the human parade replace television and movies. There'd be no reruns, anyway, and after they eventually died, I'd have *new* programs to watch. I'd sit in an unoccupied chair, nodding affably and rooting *for* this person whom I'd cast as hero or heroine, and *against* that person, whom I'd see as the villain in the piece. Maybe it would even be fun for me.

In a century or two.

But for now, the possibility that this house would find new owners as, I supposed, the former Zach Doyle's house had by now—that living people would move in with me—stirred fresh terrors in my soul, if I still possessed one (or ever had). It also angered me.

I mean, the living never even asked why spirits were generally found in old, deserted places like this. Did they think we'd lost all our taste or our vision when we died? It was because we knew, or soon came to know, that we were *pariahs*—jinxes; the unclean—and proud, discerning entities continue to feel shame, and know when they aren't wanted. It had been made very clear to me, remember. But there was another, a flip side of it: While the living did not give it a thought, we former people went on having a sense of property, of *ownership*. Think about it! If you succeed in enduring

175

six months, a year, in a dark hovel like this, let alone a decade or a century, it's entirely *natural* that you resent it when somebody else barges in! Incapable of speech, or sweet reason, we ghosts sometimes lose our tempers and raise hell, or the best imitation of it we can produce! If someone moved into my place, I'd be *invaded*. Trespass is a worse crime against the dead than it is against the living, you see. And if it happens, I'll do what I can to throw the interlopers *out!* I already have a few ideas on that score, let me tell you; I already know how to make myself *partly* and *partially visible*.

So it is that with infinite, measured slowness I am beginning to adjust. Not to madness *per se;* that seems a luxury to me. But simply to my lot. How I am now. One afternoon I could not remember the color of my son's eyes. The next morning—or some morning, weeks later—I could not easily recall the name of Louise's son. When more time . . . *occurs,* I'm sure I'll discover that I cannot remember the titles of my own books, nor the names of any of the characters with which I had so carefully peopled them.

Before long, I realize, I shall have no memory of who or what I have been in any manner, or whom I have known, liked or loved.

The worst part of that, I suppose, is that it doesn't scare me. It doesn't even sadden me most of the time. Not in the slightest.

Once I have forgotten it all, I will truly be the king

of all I survey—monarch, ultimate ruler, emperor of *everything!*

CHAPTER 17

"I dunno about this, man," the small boy said doubtfully, tagging still farther behind. "I'm not sure I can dig it."

"Me, too," Missy agreed, even while she shoved eagerly ahead of her brother and placed her small palms against the side of the house. Trying to peep into a window, she was miles short of being tall enough. It was almost dark and she looked tiny.

Carlos glanced back at the white boy, trying to feel cheerful and confident for Andy. Andy was the best friend he had in the whole world and they'd been pals forever—almost a week—but Carlos wished he'd stop trying to talk black. It wasn't that Carlos was offended; it was kind of a compliment, actually. But it sounded ridiculous coming from the cupid's-bow pink lips of a boy with neatly trimmed blond hair and skin paler than the snowy slush underfoot.

"You ain't gonna have to dig nothin', Andy," Carlos explained in a loud whisper. He'd decided to pretend ignorance. "We'll just open up a window and climb inside."

Grudgingly, Andy nodded. If Carlos said it was okay, it was okay. And when Carlos looked over at Missy, he had to laugh out loud, almost. Missy was at least two years younger than the boys, and when you'd never had more than nine or ten birthdays, that was like twenty years. But ole Missy was all right, she had enough adventure in her soul for all three of them. Already she'd figured out a way to get her toes in the siding and hitch herself up to the window. Her nose was smooshed against the pane as she peered inside.

"What do you see, Missy?" Carlos demanded. He'd meant to be first but she reached decisions and did things so fast it was hard to keep up with her. "Is anybody walkin' around in there?"

Missy didn't answer for a moment. Then she shook her head, soft brown curls dancing. "Nope. It's awful dark but I don't see anyone."

"Good!" Carlos nodded, satisfied. "That's what I thought. Ain't nobody lived in this here house for hundreds of years." He paused, remembering Momma's phrase. "It's made to order, people; made to order!"

He waited for Andy to ask him again, as he had a thousand times, why they wanted to go to the old house anyway. But this time Andy remained silent, hugging his arms against his sides and doing that blowey thing with his cheeks and lips. Ole Andy was his brother now, and stuff like that, but he was always cold. Once in Carlos' home, and once in Andy's and Missy's when there was nobody else there, Andy'd left his coat on while Carlos felt perfectly comfortable. Maybe there was something different about white people's blood, after all, because Carlos had never seen anybody who got as cold as ole Andy.

Motioning Missy down, he found an old crate with the sides banged in and carefully got up on the wooden frame, determined to get his friends into the house before Andy got pneumonia or something. When he tried to raise the window, it opened so quickly and so easily that it fairly shot up, nearly scaring Carlos off the crate. Nimbly, he threw one leg over the sill and dropped into the interior of the abandoned house, landing catlike and squinting cautiously into the gloom.

It seemed to be the kitchen, judging by the big double sink and outlets for appliances jutting into the room like listening devices; but he felt put off by the size of the place, exaggerated—hollowed—by its emptiness. His room, Gramp's and part of Momma and Daddy's bedroom could have been stuck into this vast space, and this was nothing but the kitchen.

Something squiggled its way across the floor at Carlos' feet and he instinctively yanked back his foot, scarcely smothering a scream of panic.

"She-it," Carlos said aloud. To redeem himself, he said it louder: *"She-it!"*

"What did you say, Carlos?" Andy's voice called from the other side of the open window. "Is somebody in there with you, man?"

Carlos sighed, turned to look out the window. Missy was reaching up to him with fists like doughnuts and eyes so bright she lit up the early night sky. Andy, several careful feet away, didn't look much bigger. "Nobody is here but us chickens," Carlos called softly with a laugh. Gramp used that expression a lot and Carlos always grinned when he heard it. He took Missy's closest hand and heaved. "Come on inside, sister chicken!"

While Missy raced across the floor to wash her hands in the sink, Carlos helped Andy and found it harder. He hadn't noticed before, but the little blond boy was sort of *fat*, when you took a good look—or a good pull! By the time Andy had joined them, Missy'd found out there was no water and looked put-upon.

"My hands are dirty and I got smudges on my good dress," she said from across the room, looking both aggrieved and suprised. She scratched her forehead, leaving another smudge.

"Missy, I told you t' change clothes if you were comin' with us," Carlos said wearily, almost paternally. Andy caught his eye with a brotherly shrug and a masculine what-can-you-expect expression. But there was something else in Andy's face, too, and Carlos knew immediately what it was.

Fear. He felt it, too, even though he knew he didn't dare show it—the fear that any children might experience in a deserted mansion blocks from home, on their own.

Except Carlos knew very well that neither Andy nor Missy felt what *he* did: vibrations on the air—currents that weren't meant to be there—*ripples* of intelligent emotion that could be traced to someone or something *else*.

And for a moment, Carlos wondered just what he thought he was doing. There was a distinct danger in being a person who dwelled more than most in the illusory right hemisphere of the brain—a small boy who had come to prefer the unseen things like ideas, beliefs, stories and the special gifts of God. While you might be aware of fine fantasies or even frightening ones that other people could not detect, you also lacked the more ordinary appreciation of practicality that motivated someone like ole Andy. And when you wove your tales of magic and shared with the Andys of the world the glimpses of invisible possibilities, and caused them to *follow* you, you had to be responsible, the way Gramp was, and be ready for leadership.

Trouble was, Carlos had been to see the shrink a second time and he knew that no one could stop that Doctor Sapers from cutting his fine powers down to pea-size, and mashing them right out of him, no one except his new best friends. When he'd decided to run away, therefore, to go somewhere else to live and keep all his magic for Andy and Missy, until it grew big and strong enough that *nobody* could shrink it down to a pea, it had seemed natural to ask them if they wanted to run away too.

And, of course, they'd said yes.

Even now, Carlos thought, edging his way toward the door leading out of the huge kitchen, he might have just left this old barn of a house and taken his buddies home except for what he'd read in Daddy's mind: that unless a change happened fast, unless he stopped reading folks' minds or making things move, Daddy was going to let Doctor Sapers have him. It was Momma's idea, Carlos realized, feeling desperately astonished and even more desperately sad, but it was *real*—it was a *fact* in the lives they led. And what his parents had decided was absolutely plain: stop being Carlos anymore or go to live in a big place with Doctor Sapers and a bunch of crazy people.

That was when he'd decided he'd rather remain himself and live here with his friends.

By the time they had crept through the dining room and then explored most of the living room—it hadn't taken long, since there was very little of anything left in the way of furniture, and none of the children knew a thing about architecture—Carlos was immensely relieved, even happy. The fear shared by the three of them was gone, and his own plan began to look better and better to him. It was chilly in here, sure (Andy hadn't even unbuttoned his coat) but that was only because it was winter. And right behind winter, Carlos knew, came spring! They might be a little uncomfortable for awhile, but there was a hundred places to play and each of them could have his or her own room, if that was what they wanted. He'd never *seen* such a big old house in his life, never even known such places were built—and one of the best parts was what *nobody* knew where they'd gone! Why, he'd even blocked out Gramp himself so *he* wouldn't know about the plan!

Missy slid down the bannister, squealing with joy, and Carlos folded his arms across his chest, feeling proud. He felt Andy's elbow against his ribs and turned, surprised by what he saw: Even old Andy was having a fine time. He was grinning from ear to ear!

"Let's explore, Carlos," Andy suggested, tugging his sleeve. "Let's go upstairs, okay? Maybe we can make a map, y' know? Put everything down so we know where it is," Andy hesitated, "man. What d' ya say?"

"I say all right!" exclaimed Carlos, holding his palms up for a high five.

Then they were running up the long, curving stairway, the ancient carpeting deadening the sound of their footfalls, little Missy tagging after them and begging for them to "Wait up." At the landing, Carlos stopped, gaping. "There must be a thousand rooms," he said breathlessly, staring into the darkness at a series of open doorways stretching out of sight. "A whole *army* must've lived here, Andy! Maybe all the soldiers from—from the Civil War stayed in these rooms!"

But Andy was impressed in a different way. Brushing at cobwebs, making a face, the look of terror had come back to his pale features. Ahead of him, where he stared in mounting anxiety, planks of shadowy blackness lay the length of the corridor, and he was imagining a movie he'd seen about men in boats and wearing eyepatches who made *other* men walk such planks to a shark-infested death. "I don't think it was the Civil War, Carlos," he whispered. "I think it was *pirates!*"

"Say what?" Carlos glanced at Missy, saw how large

her own blue eyes had grown. "You hear what he said, girl? She-*it*, there ain't no pirates alive!" He forced a bold laugh and swaggered forward. "And there ain't nobody in this house but us chickens!"

Reluctantly, the other children followed him. Now and again, floorboards screeched like banshees and cobwebs so fine they could not be seen brushed against their arms and foreheads in touches of slithering silver. Deeper into the long hallway, the shadows thickened until each child was obliged to strain to see—and increasingly, none of them wished to see what lay ahead, but dared not turn.

There was light ahead—a luminosity that seemed partly-concealed, and cupped by a hand held still; in waiting, perhaps . . .

"A c-candle," Missy said, pointing. But she kept walking.

"I'm *cold*," Andy wailed, hanging behind.

"You was *born* cold," Carlos scoffed, ashamed of how he'd lagged in the wake of the little girl. "Can't be no candle, Missy," he called, making himself talk up nice and loud to shake the terror from his limbs. "Ain't nobody here but—"

Missy was pointing again but she was standing stock still. Reaching her side, Carlos looked into her eyes and realized that the child was transfixed by fright.

With all the effort at his command, Carlos forced himself to face front—

And screamed.

That did it for the others. Andy was in the lead, shouting at the top of his lungs as he floundered back down the hallway, his chubby arms thrown out in windmilling terror. Missy caught him before reaching the stairs and, without making a sound, flashed by him and out of sight.

But Carlos hadn't budged. He was just staring, his mind closed down like an old depression-age factory. He couldn't have moved then if his life depended upon it.

The figure of a man—no, *merely the head, one arm, a single half-formed leg*—*was gliding slowly toward the boy, and Carlos could see straight through him!*

CHAPTER 18

Widowhood wasn't coming naturally to Louise Doyle, but she was doing the best she could. That had always been her way, and she had the admiring word of her late husband Zach for that.

Over the years of her two marriages, unhappy and happy, Louise often had listened to both the spoken and unspoken disaffection of aging women whose husbands were infirm. More times than not, the old women had told Louise how their mates were constantly underfoot, as if they had become drooling, balding babies immediately upon retirement. They'd implied, Louise believed, that they would be "relieved" when the "situation" changed, and she'd always found their attitude loathsome and incomprehensible.

For a long while, before Zach himself died, it had

been her hopeful notion that such wintry-souled old wives were only parroting one another, saying the odd, socially acceptable things that Americans were inclined to say. During times of dissatisfaction with government, for example, people sometimes pulled the same blanket condemnation of "self-serving crooks" over anyone and everybody in politics. Wives who rather enjoyed football sided with other wives in praying that Monday Night Football would go the way of the World Football league, say, or the American Basketball Association. They prattled about their children even when they were fully competent to discuss the world scene. And so, she thought for a time, it was with women whose husbands were dying.

She had changed her mind. It began changing a few years before Zach's demise when her best friend's father passed away and the mother, announcing "he'd have wanted it this way," promptly took off for a European vacation. She'd returned with a European husband, and the two of them had gone through her late husband's money within a year.

Her mind had fully changed after Zach's death, because while her handful of acquaintances had been supportive and outwardly understanding at the time, they'd vanished for weeks afterward, then began telephoning to urge this or that eligible male upon her. When she'd attempted to explain that she thought it was too soon, her friends tended to reply, "Of *course*, there's the matter of propriety—but you don't want to let any good bets get away!"

Even when she'd gone into detail, the other women

found it incomprehensible: that she missed Zach dreadfully; that she had truly *loved* him.

One day in late February, however, Louise awakened in a strange mood. It did not surprise her, since she knew herself well and had been expecting the mood for quite some time. Fundamentally, it was one of finality; she knew, as she fixed a solidary breakfast and listened to the din of silence breaking against the walls, that it was time to begin a new life in earnest.

If she possessed a talent of any kind, which Louise had told Zach she didn't, it was her own brand of resourcefulness. She remembered, as she turned the eggs in the skillet and added two small slices of bacon, what else he'd told her: that all her strengths were derived from an unflinching acceptance of who and what she was. Other women might survive by convincing themselves they were petite and helpless when they were actually adroit at calculating every last detail of a plan; other women won out by surprising themselves with skills they'd never known they had.

But Louise, in Zach's opinion, was a survivor because she never deceived herself or anyone else. And her particular kind of resourcefulness arose from that.

He'd admired it, she remembered, sitting quietly in the breakfast nook and gazing out of the window, because he saw the two of them as ideally mated. They were exactly alike in many of their tastes and convictions; but where there were distinctions, her essential grasp on reality complemented his more imaginative approach to life. Louise smiled as she sipped her morning Diet Pepsi, the soft-drink habit being the one teenage trait she still permitted herself. Most people would not have considered Zach a romantic, but she knew that it was precisely in his concept of their marriage that he had been a hopelessly sentimental poet.

By and large, he'd been right, about the marriage, and about her. While he'd never adequately defined her flair for being resourceful, Louise had. Many persons performed well if the blows they took were either infrequent and light so they could be regarded as "minor setbacks," or if they were positively battered to the ground, devastated. After all, the only direction was up.

But while she had been limited by a marital financial foundation that remained wobbly and unstable to the last, Louise knew that her resourcefulness was as middleclass or middle-level—and therefore as special, as individualistic—as she herself. When Zach was alive, she'd prided herself, without discussing it aloud with him or even her mother, upon sensing when things were going sour. At times when Zach's books were selling, she'd been able to see that there were other kinds of fiction he should be writing. When they were joyfully spending the money he'd earned as an advance, or a rare royalty check, she'd always known that magic moment when they needed to tug on the reins and begin holding on to the money they had left.

Her regret this late winter morning when random signs of spring met her solitary view was that she had almost never *said* anything about those most resourceful intuitions. Not any more than she'd said or done anything about the way her two sons were pulling away from her, gradually becoming absorbed by unwise friendships and worse habits. There was something hypnotic, lulling, about a status quo that wasn't really all that bad; one hated to tamper with it. One was taught not to believe in hunches but to feed the old gift horse another lump of sugar.

Which was why, when she'd spoken on the phone with Mother the day before yesterday, Louise had asked her to keep both boys another month or so. Never before, she realized, would she have dared presume upon her mother that way; the proper thing to have done was beg that her sons be quickly returned to her. But while she'd have given anything to have Zach back with her, there was one way in which the experience was liberating: having no one to share problems with, she had no choice except to use her own brand of resourceful judgment at last. She wasn't in the right frame of mind to have the boys in the house, not until she'd planned a new direction for all three of them and was ready to stick with it.

As she was putting her dish and silverware in the sink, she understood that she had unconsciously decided to sell the house.

The kids needed a change, and so, since she was in the midst of one anyway, did she—a change she had sought herself. The boys had to have a chance to make new friends in a different neighborhood; please, God, there weren't dope pushers *everywhere* in America! As for Mike Abernethy, or other men she knew, Louise wasn't even sure she really wanted to date again, and the idea of remarrying, now that she was on the downhill side of forty, sounded ghastly. Part of her customary self-understanding was that she probably was a woman who was born to be married, but one who'd never been cut out for dating. Everything about it seemed so phony, and so pressure-packed.

Mike himself had not asked for a second date, in any case. He'd phoned a few times, always briefly, swiftly explaining that he was awfully busy. Each time she had sensed his nervousness, his tension, the way he sounded more like a friend of the family than a prospective lover. It was clear that he felt guilty about the way he'd fled the bedroom without even seeing to her security, the night of the haunting.

Louise was of two minds about the lanky lawyer's weak-willed performance. On the one hand, she could understand fully that people who were definitely in the clutch of panic did not behave rationally and, since he was not her husband and had made no pretense that he loved her, it had been natural for Mike to put *numero uno* just where it belonged: in first place.

On the other hand, however, she was fairly sure she could never forget how positively ludicrous he'd looked when the door flew open, and later when he'd sort of *hopped* out of the bedroom!

In a way, Louise had decided, she was rather grateful for the haunting. (That was what she called the frightening experience to herself, even though she had tried for days to imagine an alternate explanation before simply accepting it, Louise-style, for what it had seemed.) She'd hated the notion of having to fake an orgasm. Everything about the idea of being naked and pawed by her late husband's high school buddy had been a turn-off. The one reason she'd even let Mike Abernethy come upstairs was because she did know him well, she'd felt confused and lonely, and an affair with Mike would have been less like dating, more like being married.

The funny thing was that, for a week or more after that peculiar night, she had almost looked forward to the ghost's return. It had nearly killed her, Louise was fairly sure of that, but somehow she'd had the impression that the ghost wasn't really malicious as much as upset over something.

During that afternoon, having finally made satisfactory arrangements with a realtor chum of Mike's to start showing the house in a few days, she reflected about the haunting. With some difficulty she confessed to herself that she'd had the strange impression, even before the night of its frightening manifestation, of another . . . *presence* . . . in the house. She'd chalked it up to an unconscious desire for Zach to return from the grave, or at least to communicate with her, to let her know that an afterlife existed and that he'd safely made it. Made it, she prayed, to another world in which basically gentle, creative souls could work at their art, their craft, without needing to put a price tag on everything.

And then there had been a short period of time when she'd sensed a stark, abject emptiness in the house, as if any trace of Zach that might for awhile have been trapped there had reluctantly moved on, drifted out the door or perhaps through the walls themselves, because she'd never called out to it, never acknowledged her own feeling by *speaking* to the spirit. For the simple reason that modern American people did not *do* such things, did not talk to people who could not be seen, unless they harbored a secret wish to be carried off to the funny farm. Most of the people on earth believed in a life after death, or said they did; large numbers of them believed it was possible for the soul to be temporarily earthbound, what was termed a "ghost", but if you *acted* on such a belief, instead of reading or talking about it, everyone considered you neurotic, at best.

It was only in the past few days, generally when she was in bed alone, trying to sleep, that Louise had begun to feel that *something else*—another spirit, maybe, or Zach's ghost coming home—was once more in the house with her.

It was after a small supper that she again had the uncomfortable impression of an entity—an *identity*—she could not see.

The drapes at the picture window were not closed all the way and Louise noticed it was dark earlier tonight. She couldn't even make out the cars which passed the house with a sound of gasping, and the trees in the yard looked like scratches on a negative. Tense in her front room chair, she tried not to look across at where Zach usually had sat. He'd willingly shared so much with her. If she let imagination go, she'd almost be able to see his familiar outline, the shape of his clothes and incongruously aggressive nose, taking form.

But she knew it was only her imagination because that was when she realized as she began drumming her fingertips on the arm of her chair that if there was another presence, another force, in her home then, *it wasn't Zach's*. No. For one thing, there were no noises like the ones on the night of the haunting—loud, frantic, overt sounds, the kind an unseen person might produce out of sheer frustration. In fact, this night there were no noises at all, not the kind, at least, that a person generally accepted as meaningful sound. We blocked out the furnace, the water heater, and the scuttling bugs; perhaps we blocked out the sound of the earth itself when it inhaled, and turned. No, if there was anything with Louise tonight, it was trying very hard to keep its activity at a furtive level just above the subliminal. It was a borderline, a marginal hint of movement, the kind that was surely intended to set one's nerves on edge.

And cause one to arise. And seek it out.

Louise arose, but not to search for the slight suggestion of a presence. She'd never been one to go out of her way to find trouble; trouble was the best hounddog in all creation. She stood because the wind was picking up outside and she knew that a steady, dogged rain must have begun beating down on the portion of the roof Zach had meant for months to repair. By now it was leaking through; and so she retrieved a cooking pan from the kitchen, meaning to climb the stairs to the second floor and place it directly beneath the bedroom leak.

If this kept up, Louise ruminated as she headed toward the stairway, she'd have to replace the entire roof. That was costly. Thus, her decision to sell was reinforced by a mindless drip. Perhaps she would simply bypass all such irksome problems by taking the initial offer for the house, then move into an apartment. Everything in life was a mixed blessing, and while one had to worry about being especially quiet in an apartment, as opposed to a house, she also . . .

Two steps up, she felt the presence—or *a* presence—*staring at her.*

Holding the pan as if it were a weapon, she turned back toward the front room—and saw the face, from the other side of the picture window. A face that appeared to have no features except for two white, bulging, gaping eyes.

One hand went to her pounding breast as the face disappeared.

Then she heard someone knocking at the door.

For a long moment, after going to it, she stood stock still, trying to get her breath and stop the pain inside. Ghosts did not rap at the door, despite an eerie favorite story of hers called "The Monkey's Paw." Neither, most of the time, did rapists. *Most* of the time.

Wishing passionately that they had a front door with a pane of one-way glass, she found the courage to put out a faintly shaky hand and, after a tremulous, final pause, to turn the knob and pull the door open.

A weathered, black, masculine face was visible in the viciously slicing rain, the lips moving. Louise was so frightened it took her another second to grasp what the old man was saying: "Miz Doyle, you got to tell me, please: *Where is your husband?*"

CHAPTER 19

Andy was half a block away before he realized it was pouring rain, and even then it didn't occur to him to be cold the way he usually pretended, because it had been such a neat way to get attention.

He saw his sister Missy turning back to him, all breathless after a run of terror that was awfully long for an eight-year-old girl, and he thought for a minute that she was crying. The possibility was more surprising to Andy, if not actually spookier, than what had happened in the old house. He was too young and too much boy to know if he loved his sister or not, but he sure did admire her. Ever since he'd watched Pop pull her tooth with a string, maybe a year ago, Missy hadn't shed a single tear. She hadn't made a scene, or got mad, or done anything but kind of roll through life and Andy wondered if taking away her tooth might have turned her into stone.

But the tears streaking the roundcheeked face were raindrops instead, and he approached her on the sidewalk warily, wondering why she'd stopped running. If he hadn't have been almost out of breath, too, he'd have run straight home.

"Carlos is in there," she said.

Andy, for good reason, did not consider himself a master of the quick quip. "Who?" he asked, stalling.

Missy raised a gloved hand. There was a hole in the thumb, from where she'd sucked and chewed on it, and now she was pointing her index finger at the dark mansion, at the second floor, actually. Andy followed it with his eyes. "Carlos is still there," she said simply.

He flew instantly into a tower of boyish rage. "It was his idea!" *Stomp* with one foot, in the middle of a rain puddle. "I didn't *want* to go!" *Stomp* with the other in a second puddle. He looked down at his wet feet, and the sidewalk. The rain was patiently refilling the little valleys. "I ain't goin' back," he said sullenly.

"Carlos is a good dude," Missy replied calmly, her voice fading.

When Andy looked up, panicky, he saw that she was striding with the same purposeful walk of their mother, who'd singlehandedly acquired over one hundred signatures on her ERA petition.

Andy made several noises at the back of his throat, watching Missy go. Almost instantly she became a little speck against the backdrop of the crumbling old building. She made him think of the tales he'd read about mice which disabled elephants and rabbits who outsmarted foxes with razor-sharp teeth. She made him think about Sunday School, and David using the modern technology of his time to topple Goliath. She made him think about having to to go the bathroom.

"Wait up, Missy!" he shouted, half-running and half-waddling after the small figure. Already she was at the side of the yard, atop the hill, scrambling onto the half-demolished crate. He caught up, puffing and pretending to laugh. "I was just jokin'," he assured her.

"I know," Missy assured him, nodding her head and looking very wise. "I knew you'd come."

It wasn't until they were inside the great house again, nearing the wide stairwell with the ornate bannisters, that Andy said, "I'm *cold!*"

But Missy didn't reply. She knew he would stay, now that he was with her again, where he belonged. Cautiously, Andy pressing close, she began her ascent into blackness.

The thudding rainfall made distant rapping sounds as it fell upon the roof. Total darkness had fallen so rapidly that it was as if a hand had tugged down a curtain. It was almost impenetrable as they climbed. Neither child was able to see much. Missy strained to make out the way the big steps with the mouldering carpeting curved; and Andy, inches behind her, tried only to keep his sister in view. She had removed her coat for reasons of her own, and he yearned to reach out for the big blue bow at the back of her dress and hold on.

But when they'd reached the landing, avoiding most of the creaking places their feet had found before, the luminosity down at the end of the hallway seemed peculiarly brighter than it had. It wasn't that it gave off much helpful light, actually, Andy saw; details in the peeling wallpaper and in a series of ancient Oriental rugs were no clearer than they'd appeared before. The luminosity was simply more noticeable, *stronger*, almost as if it begged them to hurry, to *come* to it. It ran off around the wooden frame of the open door as they approached. Even Missy's determined step faltered a dozen feet from the beckoning door, and Andy began blinking fast. Walking the length of the hallway was like being in the belly of some mammoth creature, like Pinocchio in the whale; he had the impression of trailing along an impossible *spine*, each open door off the corridor another nerve-laden vertebra of the sleeping beast. But passing through the illuminated doorway was entering the very *head* of it, crawling up into its brain, where the creature's nerve-center twitched and its hating red eyes would *see* and give the ultimate command to the rest of the body: *digest!*

Missy stepped into the room and Andy followed.

Carlos, cross-legged, was sitting on the floor of the room. His back was to them, and he wasn't moving.

And standing above Carlos, towering there, the spiderswept window on the other side of the room clearly visible through the apparition's chest and abdomen, was the ghost. One pale hand was raised to them.

"Yo!" cried Carlos, his voice cheerful. He hadn't turned to see them, not with his eyes. "Come on in! I want you t' meet my friend!"

CHAPTER 20

"You haven't by any chance seen a little boy around here? A little black boy?" Old Pete was intense, after the woman finally asked him in out of the rain, but he tried not to seem desperate. She hadn't known who he was and he'd had to explain about that time he and his family did some hauling work for her. But he'd seen the expression of terror on her white face at once, and hadn't taken her rudeness personally. Besides, there just wasn't time for that kind of feeling. "He was with my boy and me—'bout so high, with big eyes and a nice, friendly grin?"

Louise shook her head, tried to regain her breath. She murmured "no," but when she was tired or overwrought, she sometimes failed to project her voice. For the life of her, she hadn't been able to recall this pleasant-faced old gentleman until he'd mentioned

Zach's office in the garage. Now, as the memory returned, it seemed to her at least a year ago.

She realized that she was behaving very rudely and stood up straight. What would the old man think of her! "He's your grandson, you say? What is his name?"

"Carlos," Pete replied at once, leaning forward with apprehension. How many little black boys could she have seen in this neighborhood? "That was the name of my daughter-in-law's grandfather, and Alma Jo always liked it." Her Spanish *white* grandfather, he thought, knowing how Alma Jo was. "Have you seen him?"

"Why, no." Louise flushed. "I'm terribly sorry. I didn't mean to create any false hopes, and it isn't *you* who—" She stopped, inhaling, getting a grip on her nerves. "I'm afraid there haven't been any unfamiliar youngsters in the neighborhood recently. Not that I've noticed, anyway. But why would he come here?"

Old Pete sighed, picked at the bright feather in his hatband. "Miz Doyle, that's such a long story, I don't rightly believe we has the time for it." He looked up at her suddenly, his aging features mournful. "Ma'am, I mean you and your family no harm. All I wants is to get my little grandson home safe. Would you be kind enough to answer the question I asked you at the door?"

Louise paused, vaguely startled. She had reached the conclusion that she'd simply misunderstood the old man, lost his words in the swirl of rain and her own recurrent terror. "You want to know where my husband is? Well, he's . . . dead."

"Yes, ma'am," Pete said, bobbing his head, "and

where *is* he? Miss Doyle, I don't mean his *spirit*. I mean his—mortal remains."

Her eyelids narrowed. "How in heaven's name can knowing that assist you in locating Carlos?"

Old Pete paused, thinking hard. One way to get this woman to understand, if she was at all receptive, was to send a series of thought-pictures into her mind. He felt she was open to that; he knew, by now, that she'd sensed the presence of poor Zachary Doyle when he'd been in the house but hadn't known enough to speak to him. And it might have been so different for all of them if she had; if she wasn't so modern, like Alma Jo and like Orville craved to be.

But he also could see that the white women wasn't well, and how she might take an influx of amazing pictures—a gallery of death, and afterdeath—Old Pete couldn't be sure. He cleared his throat.

"I met Mr. Doyle," he began. "The day we was all here workin'."

"But I don't understand. He was already *dead*, then—gone."

Nicely, Pete, he cautioned himself. "Yes'm, that's true, but so's what I said. Miz Doyle, I'm an old man. I seen a lot of things in my time. And I tried to learn, to accept what I saw." He smiled, giving her the lightest interior impress of his genuineness. "Your mister was here, and yes, he survived death. But—well, he has some problems."

"Problems?" Louise repeated, floundering. "How can he—? You're sure his—his spirit exists? *Lives?*"

He loved the fact that she was glad to hear it. "Oh, yes, ma'am!" He offered a firm nod. "But y'see, I was the only one to know he was here and that's why your husband asked me to help him. Afore I knew it, my little grandson Carlos wanted to help too. You know how kids can be."

She waggled her fingers, trying to find time to absorb what he was saying. She was dazzled by it, not miserably but with a confusion that contained at its heart her first true feelings of uplift since Zach's death. But the questions she might have asked would not come to mind and what the old man meant by kids wanting to be of assistance, well, that was not in her experience. "Are you saying, then, that Carlos may have left his house to look for my husband's *ghost?*"

"Well, now, that's close enough." He jiggled the old hat in his hands, beaming. But he had to take care; he was sure Carlos' life depended upon learning where the dead Mr. Doyle had been laid to rest. "Y'see, I know a old woman, name of Miz Latitude. And she gave me some ideas, even—some *things*. Things to help your late husband. I believe I can free him up to go on to Paradise, and also find Carlos." He finished his tale simply enough, his eyes pleading with her as he glanced up. "Will you tell me where I'll find Mr. Doyle's grave?"

"Wait here." She arose, so quickly it dizzied her, hurried out to the dining room and poked through her purse. She returned at a slower pace with a square of cardboard, like a greeting card. She pressed it into the reaching hand of the eager old man. "The cemetary gave me this. A map of directions. It—marks where my Zach is buried." Louise swallowed. "I haven't been able to afford the tombstone yet."

Pete, turning away, began murmuring his thanks. Then he stopped, hat still in hand, before the widow. Once, he'd have been like a great, bronze statue to her and she might never have admitted him to her home; not at night, surely. Now they were almost of a height; Peter sensed that his frailty matched hers. "Whatever happens now, ma'am," he said carefully, "I am tryin' to help. Please remember that. Old Pete wants just what's best, for his family and for his friends."

"God bless you, Pete," she said softly, and squeezed his hand.

"Why, ma'am," he responded with a toothy grin, "He *has!* A lot more times than a poor old man can even count."

By the time he'd manuevered his truck onto East 38th Street, Pete felt like humming. The beat-up old Memory Van seemed to know the way. Despite the drenching rain, and the strain on its laboring old windshield wipers, it virtually vaulted into the sparse flow of traffic heading west and he patted the steering wheel the way another man might have caressed his pet dog.

Old Pete had a theory about the Memory Van, the way he did most things. Even without knowing it, the folks who made things which *moved*—cars, ships, airplanes of this wonderful day, even bicycles, motorcycles, maybe skates and skateboards—did everything they could to endow their creations with life. That was why owners generally called them "she" and sometimes named their vehicles; that was why so many of their faithful motion-machines were named for animals; and why the vehicles' front ends appeared to have faces.

But that was just the first part of creating them; the other part was up to the folks who *owned* them. And if those folks kept them clean, looked out for their health, fed them the finest kind of fuel for their species, why, things like Old Pete's Memory Van practically *did* come to life!

Now, the primary duty a man had to his vehicle was a lot simpler. He had to keep it awhile—eight, ten, fifteen years—and pump a measure of his own self into his truck, motorcycle, or boat. He had to get to know it, pat and talk with it, learn all about its special ways, just like he had to learn about his woman. Trouble with modern times was a man didn't keep his truck, or his woman, long enough to see how she differed from others, how she was special and specially *his*. True ownership came slow; but if a man was lucky, it grew into a partnership. Pete had known many a morning when it was so cold he'd hated getting up, but the old Memory Van turned over loyally and got all charged up while younger fellows' sleek new automobiles just sat at the curb or in the driveway, yawning.

One of the grand discoveries, the old man thought as he glimpsed Throne Hill Cemetery through the lashing rain, one of his best, was how love always was a possibility with anything and everything. If a person remembered that, then reached out to show he was ready to give some of it himself, he might bring almost anything to life.

Turning into the main road of the cemetery, he felt gravel crunch beneath the tires, pulled off on a berm and paused beneath a light to read the directions given him by Louise Doyle. It had been plain awful, going to see her, scaring her so. It had been worse, knowing he could surely locate Carlos by coming to this land of the dead but being a whole lot less sure he could free poor Mr. Doyle. He'd done more than his portion of thinking lately and found, for the first time in memory, that he wasn't really positive his powers—his gifts—were a blessing. He didn't much like the way things was today, but he couldn't change them and it was doubtful Carlos could when he grew up. Pete sighed. Maybe he'd try to *unteach* the boy, the way Orville had managed to lose his own small smidgen of gifts. Or maybe he wouldn't.

But he knew for a fact that no little boy had any business running around on his own in a big city, and that no one else was going to find Carlos in time except him.

No other vehicles seemed to be present in the cemetery. It was quiet but for the rumble of the Memory Van and the rain coming down. Turning his head, Pete saw that the downpour was slowing and, by squinting, he could perceive a path leading toward the Doyle plot. He turned the key in the ignition, heard the faithful motor cough and die. Hard to tell just how deep into the wooden area the grave would be, but Old Pete decided to get out and walk.

Twelve steps down the path, his booted feet sinking in the mud, he entered a clearing and found himself atop the slope of a slight hill. His nostrils informed him he was there before his eyes, unaccustomed to the gloom, could do the job; because the newly dead rested here, and the scent of freshly turned earth was strong on the wet air. Special senses alerted, Old Pete looked down. Here and there, opened but unoccupied graves waited, the scattered dirt giving them the appearance of rude beds with the blankets pulled back.

That was when his inner ear caught the sinister murmur of distant voices, and an improbable subterranean sound almost like that of breathing . . .

CHAPTER 21

The day began exceedingly well, even memorably, for stouthearted Chauncey Wells. And that, the angel knew, was a distinct novelty for almost anyone awakening in Hell. Bouncing out of bed with spirited agility—a neat enough trick for a personage of his corpulence and preference for refinement of the intellect—he'd showered instead of tubbing. That choice had been made more because he was in a rush than for the standard reason: unfamiliar hostels, life-side, might be justifiably notorious for running out of hot water, but here, the specific challenge was how to avoid being scalded.

Ministering spirits of Chauncey's noble station could neither experience pain nor death, but each of them had sworn a perpetual oath to tolerate discomfort, and Wells thought he looked positively absurd whenever his ample flesh became mottled with crimson, like one of the chubby cherubim taking Vocation I in the cloudier heavenly clime.

What made this morning at the Hotel Hades special to him was an idea that had occurred while the obese angel was attempting to sleep. The twanging stridency of rock guitar, piped into every suite and cubicle on the guest level, had made resting an impossibility. If he'd turned on the TV he'd have received more of the same or aged reruns of "My Mother, the Car," "LaVerne & Shirley," or "The Devlin Connection." But this time, tossing and turning finally had worked to his advantage.

Wells tingled with anticipation even while, ignoring the snide remarks from the switchboard operator, he phoned in his arisal prayer. He might be wrong again but he really didn't think he was! Slipping into a newly pressed white suit, grimacing his grudging appreciation for Hell's remarkable dry-cleaning, he could not restrain a smile. At long, long last, he had an effective threat with *teeth* in it, to hold under Newton Link's aloof nose, and he rather hoped that the threat would take a bite right out of the *distingue* proboscis!

Rolling out into the corridor of the corporate living quarters, the circular seraphim arranged his moon face, striving for the proper balance between absolute disdain for the evil place and a spot of something benign, something with a modicum of winning hope. Unfortunately, a glance told Wells how unlikely it was that he'd made any converts today. Hundreds of the beautiful Misses for Mammon, also euphemistically called "hostesses" by the Management, were closing doors behind them, giggling at the parting remarks made by the satanic staff they'd just finished servicing. For a second, Wells paused to peer disapprovingly at the lovely horde, conscious of how many of them he could identify by face or other highly-publishable accoutrements. He observed that many of them, either for penalty or simple recognition, had the name of an earth month stenciled into their soft shoulders. *That February*, he thought, mentally taking a step after her, *she's the absolute image of dear old Lady Borille-Ecce!*

But now wasn't the time to try to strike up old acquaintances, however delightful it might be to err . . .

Hell offered a solid, boiled breakfast which often appealed to Wells but he resisted the temptation with practiced ease and walked briskly toward Newton Link's offices. If Wells understood the handsome imp at all, Link was fit to be tied this morning. That adorable little chap, young Carlos, had located the spirit of Zachary Edson Doyle and by tonight he'd surely have the fellow feeling top-rung—absolutely aces!

Of course, Newton would tend to place the blame upon his own fleshy shoulders, Wells saw, for causing the boy to leave home and then steering him to Zach; but that wasn't the precise truth of the situation at all. It was true that Wells had seen to it that kind old Pete remembered their obvious obligation to the Creator for the psychic skills given them. But he had not interfered in any way whatsoever in the way that Carlos and his grandfather defined their mortal gratitude. It had been adequate, Chauncey reflected smugly, as he passed through an office pool of unquestionably the worst typists in the whole universe, to remind them of Him from whom all blessings—mixed or otherwise—flowed.

Just as Chauncey had been sweetly helpful when he recommended to Link that some of these fumble-fingered young women in the office pool be given a secondary task of learning the function of a computer. It wasn't *his* fault if Link had forgotten how the pretty secretaries got their life-side jobs, or why their former employers grieved for them so much. And it wouldn't be *his* fault when the desirable new DP people got the hellish hardware so confused that Link and his peers forgot even to pay off on overdue wish-pacts!

None of which would help convince Zach Doyle's shade to return to his former home, and climb the garage steps to his empty den, where heaven itself awaited him. That, Chauncey sensed, could not now be affected except as the product of this morning's brilliant idea—today's tooth-edged threat which he planned to drop upon Link with as blissfully, chortling glee as his own semi-divine soul allowed.

The deepest truth, Wells believed now, was that neither his side nor Link's would claim the Doyle spirit if he stayed in that old deserted mansion. And that genuine conviction alone empowered him to take more drastic steps, since the prolonged absence of the human soul being used by Doyle was wrecking the statistical summations of both sides.

What Chauncey Wells meant to do was to look ingenuously, innocently at Link, shrug helplessly, and issue the threat: either heaven gets to collect Doyle, by virtue of the fornicating forfeit clause—or Heaven will *resurrect* Zachary Doyle!

But when Wells wheeled past Ms. Moloch, avoiding her both because he did not wish to be delayed and because the wise soul did not look long at the office ogress, and barged into Link's private quarters, there was no one present.

Wells, in the doorway, cast an anxious glance from corner to cultivated corner. The papers still stacked on Newton's desk indicated he would not be away long, a factor of confidence that made the obese angel shudder. Although the desk computer remained, the exquisite leather attache case Link had seized from a quickly deteriorating corporate controller was absent.

Feeling something touching his shoulder, Chauncey glanced down. It was Ms. Moloch. He had to help her extricate her index claw from the shoulder of his white suit. "Yes, Ms. Moloch?" he said briefly. "What is it?"

She gazed up at him, her rows of yellow fangs forming a hideous smile. "Newton isn't here," she said gutterally.

"Yes, yes, woman," Wells grumbled, "I can see that for myself. Are you at liberty to inform me about his whereabouts, or is that a Satanic state secret?"

She looked keenly puzzled, which is to say, infinitely stupid. And indescribably ugly. Saint Peter's sinuses, *why* did Link keep this creature around! Wells held his breath, steadied his soul, and looked down into her red-lashed eyes. "Where did Link *go?*" he inquired softly.

This time she got it. When he saw the eyeless scarlet mask on the wall in her typing space, just about the size of her hirsute head, and her altogether earth-girl bosom jiggle in a forty-nine inch circumference when she nodded, Chauncey began to understand why Link kept her about.

But it was the direction in which Ms. Moloch was pointing with her claw that made Wells shiver: straight *up*.

CHAPTER 22

By the time I realized the sound I'd heard downstairs was that of a window in the kitchen opening, the intruders were stumbling through the kitchen and dining room, their calling voices stunning me. I mean that I was literally driven back against the wall in my bedroom, cringing. That astonishes you, I imagine; *they were children*, you gasp. Please let me try to explain.

Ever since moving to the mansion I had forced myself to regard as my home, a period I could not measure by any of the ordered and stately increments living man calls "hours" or "days," I had existed in a world with a different sequence of senses. Additionally, there were those of a kind I'd never believed possible when I was alive. I doubt that you would have suspected them either, but I do not wish to describe any that you cannot, yourself, imagine. You might find the very nature of them frightening, or discomfiting.

Besides, it is that new ordering of sensual prominence I want to cite, not the bizarre and otherworldly newcomers. Because I was still able to see, smell, and hear, even sometimes to will myself to touch certain objects—but in a fashion I wouldn't want my worst enemy to experience. (Mike Abernethy, perhaps, althought I could not, at that time, have remembered his name.)

You see, my day-to-day affairs were lived—please let me call it that; I have no new vocabulary and I do think of myself as "living"—in a constant narrowing process. With no one around to talk to, or hear, with nothing whatsoever to do and no desire to leave the house, I found that I was building each day an imprisoning cell in which I half-consciously confined myself. The sameness of existence soon became simultaneously the source of all my comfort and the source of all I dreaded most. Psychologists tell us that even normal, living beings sometimes transfer the helpless anger they feel for a person of authority to an object or possession, even a more helpless person, upon which the anger can be spent. It is, you can see, a cleansing solace for the angered individual if not for the things or persons on whom he expends his wrath.

Well, in a way, I believe that's just what I did to the huge, unfeeling house. I'd reached the stage of overflowing with old anger and stale frustration toward the unfeeling entities who had failed to come for me. But if I could transfer those feelings to the mansion, my home, by limiting my appearance in this room or that, by withholding my periodic kingly displays of pompous madness, by ignoring the spider in the kitchen and refusing to feed the family of mice, I was enabling myself to use up some of my sick fury. Being a ghost, I found, was an utterly, appallingly selfish proposition.

What I *didn't* see was the dismal extent to which I had become an integral part of the house, like the closets or windowglass, so that I began punishing myself as well. Lying on the unmade bed, chattering at absolutely nothing—or walking *almost* into the kitchen, so that the mice and the spider knew I was there but tossing my head as I turned to stride nobly away—I was narrowing the threshold of my senses by the minute. I began, while in bed, staring at the design imprinted in the wallpaper and soon counted all the lines in the basic print, then attempted to total all the designs in the bedroom. After what I suppose was a week or more of that, my vision turned into a single, infinitely thin line that, when I finally left the room to prowl the dark hallways, took me on a tightroping course that did not see another living thing to my left or right.

Which leads me back, almost, to the noise of the intruders in my kitchen. You see, my hearing was doing much the same thing as my vision—not to such a conscious degree, but with similiarly drastic effect.

The old house was erected atop a hill at the back of the lot, if I forgot to mention that. By virtue of simple distance, sounds from the street were somewhat muted. Add to that the impervious thickness of the walls—they really knew how to build houses, one hundred years ago! —and the fact that there was never much traffic on this particular side street, and you have a picture of almost complete auricular isolation.

Add to all the foregoing the fact that I did not, upon arriving here, *want* to hear the noises of normality because they added up to a cacophony of alienation which at the time made my soul ache like an infected tooth.

Yet people, living or dead, have a way of unconsciously wanting to use each of their senses, sooner or later. I'd read an astrology article once arguing that "earth sign natives"—Taurus, Virgo and Capricorn—were nearer to nature than other people, and one of the more obvious commands of human nature was, *Eat*. That was why such men and women tended toward heaviness. The same piece stated that "water sign natives"—Cancer, Scorpio, and Pisces—were closer to courses of human emotion than other persons, and that since sexuality was arguably the most intense of emotional drives, such people formed stronger desires for, or aversions to, sex than most men and women.

Eventually, quite consciously, I needed to *hear* something, but only rarely could I discern the sound of my own voice.

And spiders do not make a lot of noise. I recall sitting on the floor in the kitchen, from the instant I saw late winter daylight struggling past the window until it was black as pitch in the room, keeping tabs on my friend, the spider.

Now I know what they say about dogs, when UFOs are hovering in the sky—that so-called lower animals have the knack for sensing the coming of alien life; that it is often they who growl softly, thereby notifying their masters. Although I am only recently an alien upon this planet of my birth, the effect may be similar and I would swear that *my* spider did not know he had a master. Or a friend. Because it finally crept into plain view, then unhesitatingly raced upon those small, uncanny legs until it panted against my index finger and the nail of my thumb. It didn't do any kind of doubletake; it didn't freeze. It simply went on about its arachnidial affairs as if an invisible being of monumental size, from its vantage point, had not in his frustration attempted to squash it.

It moved soundlessly away. I know, because I remained there after it was dark, trying to hear that goddamned bug make even the slightest noise. I didn't.

I found it easier to make friends with the mice. Sometimes, if I used my mind to make a scrap of paper flutter to their hole in the wall, one or two members of the family—probably the kids, curious and bolder—would emerge and run across it with an absolutely delicious crackling sound. Each time it happened, I was in ecstasy. But whenever I caused the paper to soar over their tiny heads and land coaxingly in front of them, it always sent them scattering to hiding places in terror. *One* sound, one unimaginably wonderful sound, was all I was permitted, perhaps once every week or ten days. For a time, I existed to hear it again.

But by the evening when the three youngsters broke

into the house, I'd run out of patience to await my aural treat and was more or less voluntarily bedfast. At the same time, however, I'd long since trained myself in what I should do in the face of such an emergency and my reaction was instantaneous and instinctive.

I lurked inside my room, giving off a rather peculiar, yellowish illumination I had discovered in my new bag of psychic tricks, and concentrated until certain sections of my body—only *sections;* I still knew enough sound amateur psychology to know what would scare living people!—were visible. Both Spielbergian effects—luminosity and partial visibility—were strictly temporary, of course. I'd found they took a great deal out of me, principally in terms of my ability to remember some of the details of my previous corporeal existence. While there were still those occasions when I attempted to go mad, much of the time I saw it as a matter of pride to keep touch with the past. I knew that I'd been a writer of some kind, that I'd lived elsewhere in the same city with a pretty woman I loved, that her name was Lou Ann, or Louisa, and that we'd had a child. And a dog, a large dog.

But while I waited for the intruders to come and discover old hideous me, I lost all that in the pressing need to frighten the bejesus out of the people climbing the stairs. They were, I became convinced with every step, here for a dark purpose—to buy the house from the realtors who'd given up years ago on ever unloading such an unluscious lemon; to occupy the place, to *move in to my house,* and thereby shake me out of the self-limiting cell of the senses which was my horror and yet my only way of remaining sane.

Why didn't I recognize the whispers and the sudden, sharp speeches in the hallway as the voices of children? Because, I suppose, I'd entered the stage of a certain psychic senility; because I'd completely forgotten what children *sounded* like.

And when I saw them, the pale-skinned ones immediately turning to run from me (a scene that brought me, at once, a rollercoaster ride of internal ambivalence) and the darker skinned one who confronted me, I'll admit that my first reaction was ridiculous.

I believed that I had grown. That I'd become the giant that the spider and the family of mice believed me to be—or *would* have considered me, if they'd had any notion that I was there.

Now, I wonder, would I have done harm to the little black boy if he hadn't spoken? Candidly, I have enough humanity left that I hope I wouldn't, but I can't swear to it. When Carlos' beautiful eyes rolled back and he found the remarkable courage to smile at me, most of the sanity I was trying to protect was sheerly a matter of imagination.

Then he said, clear as a bell, "*I* know you! You're Mr. Doyle!"

And I seriously doubt that he ever knew, the rest of his life, what an indescribably mervelous favor he did for me. The word "lifeline" is, of course, inappropriate. But it isn't an exaggeration.

Well, he coaxed me to sit down on the floor in front of him, and I tried to start remembering more efficiently than I'd been doing, to piece things together and to understand, among other things, how Carlos knew who I'd been.

To my amazement, the little fellow helped clear things up by dint of a gift he had for telepathy. I had only to wonder, dully, about this or that question, and without speaking Carlos would place the answer with remarkable lucidity before my mind's eye.

By the time the other two children returned for their friend, with rather more courage than most of the adults I'd known, I knew that I was well on the way toward regaining my sense of perspective as well as my memory. It took Carlos and me quite a while, but the two of us succeeded in calming Andy and Missy— those were their names—and I was suddenly in the midst of the first real conversation since my death.

Yes, I know. They were just kids and, besides that, Carlos was obliged to take the comments I'd made telepathically and pass them along to the white children in spoken words. But they were *people*, thinking, feelingful, different *people*, and I had only one regret for most of that evening— that I'd remembered the person I loved most in the world as Louisa, or Lou Ann, when "Louise" had been the last word I uttered upon my own deathbed.

After Carlos had explained the way his grandfather, the old gentleman who'd inherited my typewriter, had urged him to use his special talents for helping folks, living or dead, he tried to describe to me the way that his own people, aside from Old Pete, thought him crazy. I found my recent fury building up again, but directed this time againt anyone who would wish to change or harm such a decent, helpful, bright little boy. It seemed to me then that the wrong human beings were dying everywhere, and I continued to maintain that fiery notion when, a delightful hour or two later, the awful thing happened to Carlos.

We spent that time, the four of us—three living, one dead—playing.

I can't recall the last time I played while I was alive, and I am incapable of naming anyone I know who did. If Louise and I were obliged to visit the home of another couple, it unfailingly turned into a contest of one-upsmanship. They showed us all the new things they'd bought, from the absurdly expensive wine they poured, to a print for which they'd paid several hundred dollars—a *print!*—and from the backyard pool they were installing to a new suite in Junior's bedroom. *We*, away from home, did our best to keep up by talking about important book contracts of mine, or lying about the kids' grades. Men sometimes got together for a poker game, or couples, again, for bridge, or pinochle, but it wasn't *playing*, it was win-at-all-costs-our-reputation's-at-stake. I'd wagered money I couldn't afford on basketball games, caring not a farthing about either the team or the cash I might win, but I cared about *outsmarting* men who were supposed to be my friends.

Well, Carlos, Missy, Andy and I *played*. Part of my plan was to take away from all three children any fear of ghosts they might have—although Carlos, I saw, had none at all—and I also wanted them to notice that, while I was dead, I yet lived. Not that I was ready to be pleased about my state. I only hoped to reinforce their individual beliefs in God, in a Creator who would not forsake His duties and promises. My own faith might have turned rocky as hell, I thought, but it had nevertheless sustained me in life and I agreed with the philosopher, the one who'd said that if God didn't exist, humankind would have to invent Him.

Eventually, as was probably inevitable, Carlos and I put on a show for the other two kids. He seemed inspired by my presence and, though I was tiring badly in an effort to remain visible (I'd added my missing limbs, feeling silly about it), I was astonished by the boy's bag of tricks.

For my part, I did something I'd been wanting to do anyway. I used the psychokinetic power of my surviving mind to bring the abandoned clothes out of the closet, and make them dance. Equally inspired by Carlos, having the time of my death (if you won't mind the joke too much), I animated suits, dresses, shirts and pants until they became a veritable Bolshoi Ballet of enlivened garments! A two-piece tweek bowed gallantly before a low-cut jersey, and they jitterbugged their hearts out. An evening gown with fluffy sleeves dipped and whirled before a shiny tuxedo in a fashionable foxtrot, and two pair of faded jeans—topless—wriggled their flashless hips to an unheard but frantic disco beat.

I stopped, and they promptly fell to the floor like the victims of the infamous Dancing Madness, when pert little Missy screamed and pointed.

For a moment, only for a moment, I thought Carlos was just emulating the cavorting clothes. He had spun around twice, then thrown out his arms as if trying to clutch, to *hold on* to someone, or something.

But when I saw his face, I believed for another instant that he'd somehow become tangled in an electrical cord. Because his eyes were rolling back in his head and his mouth was moving, as if in pain. I thought of shock, believed with horror that the child who had saved me was being electrocuted.

I felt his mind groping in mine, then—I saw in my own thoughts what Carlos was seeing, somehow, and I sensed the feeling of hopelessness he had, as I watched the picture take form before my inner eye.

The picture of a lovable old black man with an expression of abject terror etched into every valiant crease of his face.

CHAPTER 23

From atop the gray rise, Old Pete stared down at the series of newly opened and recently filled graves at the foot of the hill, and surprised himself by not wishing to descend. The fact that most other people would have shared his apprehension and reluctance meant nothing at all to him. He'd seen death close-up a hundred times in his four-score-and-who-knew-how-many years and never flinched. He'd *spoken* to spirits, not only through Miz Latitude's mediumistic offices, but *direct*. He'd seen good men die, and some rascals who weren't so good, and he'd buried women whom he had grown to love awhile.

But he'd never had the impression of mortal danger he felt now.

Which warned him, when the thought occurred, that maybe what he faced, if he were to perform the tasks expected of him by God, Miz Latitude, and his own lifetime of good conscience, had to do with *immortal* danger, danger to his soul.

Briefly, the old man lifted his head, sniffed, tried to get through the odor of turned earth so pungent in his flared nostrils. The woods themselves shouldn't spook him, Pete knew, because he was a country boy by birthing and bringing up. Yet the wind whipping at his wrinkled neck and slipping its icy fingers beneath his oft-patched jacket, filled him with a new kind of dread. He felt exposed where he stood atop the hill, even if he was just a black silhouette on a moonless and rainswept night, even if he didn't know what he was exposed to. There was a nerve-provoking *nakedness* to it, because the frail old body kept no secrets from the snooping wind; and he found his thoughts ambling back through the years in search of similar situations.

As they came to mind, the old man experienced a certain chill of pleasure, and he laughed deep in his throat despite himself. Folks saw an old person, stooped and maybe getting stupid, and tended to believe that he or she had been *born* just that old—that there'd never been a day when the blood ran hot with excitement or passion, or the thrill of danger. There'd been the autumn evening when he'd lent a helping hand to a member of his sprawling makeshift "family." Cousin Mose was surviving the depression by making moonshine—plain "shine," they'd called it—and all had gone well until Mose and Pete finished loading the truck. Next up was a back-road, midnight-alley distribution of the unlabeled bottles to the cousin's anxious customers. But the government fellas, the revenuers, had caused a change in plans, and a wild, risky, thoroughly enjoyable chase Old Pete recalled to this day. There'd been the steaming hot summer's day when a bunch of rednecks had nothin' better to do than lynch Uncle Frederick, and . . .

Voices called to him, moaned their desperate need to escape corruption.

Jaw set in grim lines, the old man half trotted, half fell down the slope to the foot of the hill, stopping immediately and standing erect when the next surprise greeted him.

Here, near the yawning and freshly sealed graves, there was no trace of wind, no sound from the world beyond the cemetery. But there was warmth—unnatural, stifling *heat* and, upon the scarcely stirring air, an indefinable smell of something cloyingly sweet. None of which belonged.

Hastily, Pete plucked the cardboard with information which Miz Doyle had given him from an inside pocket, and looked for a match-up between the number on the card and the numbers rudely printed on signs which were staked to the earth. *704*, read the data on Miz Doyle's card; *704* read the legend on the sign rising from the foot of a fairly recent, sealed grave.

"I don't rightly want to do this, Mr. Doyle," Pete muttered under his breath, producing the pouch given him by Miz Latitude and opening it wide on the edge of the gravesite. Most of the drizzling rain had stopped now and the moon was starting to squirm faintly from behind its cloud cover. "But you remembers my grandson, Carlos, I knows you do. And with the good Lord's help, well, maybe I can help you to be free."

Kneeling, he said a quick prayer, then tried to remember the things that the spirit of the old woman had told him. He'd never liked voodoo in any of its forms, himself; he hadn't cared much for the people who practiced it, folks who, in the old man's view, went to church and sang hymns in the Sunday choir but dabbled in dubious magic the rest of the week. They were folks who appeared to want the best of all possible worlds. It was the semiofficial religion of Brazil, and Haiti; he knew that. But he considered it dangerous.

Still, in one sense of the word, Miz Latitude had always been as modern as next Christmas's toys. Because all that interested her, when it came down to that, was whether a thing *worked* or not. He'd never been able to be quite that practical and down to earth.

He shut his eyes for a moment. Miz Latitude had said he must appeal to the legendary Old Black Slave, a powerful spirit in Umbanda rites because his soul contained the spirits of countless dead slaves. And because the Old Black Slave had suffered greatly, he was kind and good, he loved little children, and he cared for others who had been mistreated. Pete grunted. Maybe the Old Black Slave and he weren't as different as he'd thought.

Feeling uncomfortably warm, he spread out a towel with large square blocks—the design was important—and opened a bottle of inexpensive muscatel. He poured a few drops of the wine upon a scrap of cemetery bark, then propped up the bottle, half wishing he could steal a swig. Upon the towel he set an unsmoked pipe and a packet of good tobacco as offerings.

Then Pete hesitated, unwilling to proceed. At last he took out the stub of a candle Miz Latitude had given him, lit it, and placed it between the bark and the towel. And finally, to complete the ritual, he bowed his head with a feeling of disgust and asked the Old Black Slave to keep Carlos safe and return the boy to him, and to release the spirit of the white man named Zachary Edson Doyle.

Finished, sighing, Pete arose and truded back up the hill and along the path to his Memory Van. For most folks, that would have been the easy part and what he had to do now might have seemed terrifying. Because he was going to dig up the casket, and open it—enable the Old Black Slave to answer his prayers. And if they were answered, there'd be a final portion of the ritual which Old Pete rather approved: he'd need to buy a bottle of the finest cognac and a box of the finest cigars, bring them back to the grave and leave them in payment.

From the truck bed Pete pulled a small spade he'd brought for the purpose of excavating the grave, and hoped his unreliable, aching old back would be up to it. Looking at a dead body didn't pose any serious problems. He didn't *want* to do it, he wouldn't *like* the grassy smell rising to his nostrils; but the poor man's remains were beyond doing any harm to anybody and there was no way that this could be considered grave robbing. In a robbery, you took something away. You didn't leave it; not even a prayer, or hope.

Now that Old Pete knew the location of Mr. Doyle's interment, he saw that it wouldn't take long to get back to his nocturnal labors and, since the rain had softened the ground, he hoped yet to be back home before it was much past midnight. He followed his own fairly deep tracks in the muddy earth, wondering if Miz Latitude's rites would prove as effective as usual —praying they *would be*. Carlos was the sweetest and dearest thing in the world to him; the ritual *had* to work.

But as he paused atop the rise a second time, and thought he heard once more the distant, numbing mutter of voices and a pathetic underground chorus of eerie groans, he forced himself to smile and shake his head. *I must be gettin' old*, Pete mused, *or plain soft in the brain*.

Because he had overlooked the most obvious truth in the world, one that meant there was simply no sensible reason to be afraid of this land of the dead.

Spirits might sometimes be left upon earth, for reasons that were none of an old man's business. There might be a few thousand ghosts earthbound in the nation, perhaps a million in the world; and some of them, being ex-people, might not be the nicest beings in the good Lord's wide universe.

But nobody, not even Hell's keepers, would be cruel enough to leave a human spirit six feet under ground, conscious, reasoning, hopelessly unable to move throughout boundless eternity.

Which meant, pure and simple, that the hint of talking and the whining sounds he'd believed he heard were nothing more than a combination of the wind whistling through the woods and an old man's whispering imagination.

Unhesitatingly now, Old Pete dropped back down into the realm of graves, and shook his head sadly at Number 704. Oh, mercy, what an *unhappy* thing it was, an unmarked place of burial! He hoped Miz Doyle would find the money for a nice, neat, white stone one day soon. Of course, just as he'd come to realize it himself, the holy spirit had gone on. There wasn't anybody down there but us chickens, he told himself. Or a scattering of unrecognizable white bones that might just as well have come from an old chicken! He smiled. But still, well, it was a final resting place, and the spruced-up living passed by on fine Sunday afternoons around Easter and Memorial Day, and there wasn't nothing there to say "Hello, I used to live in this city too. I was an all right person with a family and, just the way you're bound to do, I found my life had run out. But welcome, thanks for dropping by, and mend your own ways while there's time left for you."

Glancing toward the streaked blackboard of a sky, at an emerging moon which looked to him like a single, slightly bilious, watching teacher's eye, Old Pete leaned on his spade and began to dig.

He was right; it wasn't difficult dirt to bite and move to one side. It was so easy, in fact, Old Pete thought as his breathing became labored, that it was almost as if the grave had been recently dug, then filled in again. The candle burning from the lip of the deepening hole flickered occasionally, working with the errant moonlight and the rivulets of sweat to give the old man a temporary zebra's face; and then his head was beneath the surface, only the spade in his strong hands rising into view as Pete deposited further muddy dirt on the ground.

It felt good, in a way, to regain contact with nature. It surely wasn't a thing he'd care to do every day, the way he had once, as a boy, and it couldn't be good for an eighty-year-old heart. But Pete found himself humming, the melodies softly drifting up from the grave as old as he himself. Memories, too, played in his mind—swiftly seen and replaced images of the men he had worked with, the bosses who'd grudgingly paid him, the sweet, sassy ladies for whom he'd cleaned up and changed clothes on nights that seemed to shove aside the limits of time and last, for awhile, forever.

He was much too preoccupied to wonder why there was no caretaker around anywhere in the cemetery, or to ask what might have happened to him.

When the dully gleaming surface of the coffin came into view, Old Pete used the tip of the spade and his hands to level the last layer of dirt and then, working carefully, used a single gnarled finger to trace the outline of the cross.

The noise inside the casket was inescapable. Something sentient was scrabbling around in there. Something, inside a coffin buried for months, was scratching against the lid—on the other side . . .

Through his partly opened eyelids, little Carlos saw that Mr. Doyle's spirit was beginning to fade, that the ghostly outline was flickering, like a candle's disturbed flame. Even Andy and Missy had noticed it and were alarmed for poor Mr. Doyle, the way he was—because both children were on their feet, staring as the shade came perilously close to *disappearing!*

With tremendous effort, the boy shook away the frightening image of Gramp that had haunted his mind—the picture of his beloved grandfather, looking spooked out of his wits—and it was replaced by the words he'd heard Gramp utter so many times: "Your gift is for *helping* folks, and for no other reason. Remember that, boy—you has to use your powers for *good*, whether the folks is black or white, alive or dead!" And something else, words both his parents, Alma Jo and Orville, liked to say to small boys: "First things first, Carlos—*then* you can play."

He jumped to his feet, reached out with the most effective tool for helping he had in his power—his ability to plant thoughts in another's mind, to reassure them, let them know somebody cared.

The spirit eyes of Zach Doyle met Carlos', glazed, and the shade was solidly materialized once more before the three children. Then his own message took form in Carlos' mind, mystifying the boy, frightening him: *They're killing me again*, the words came; and, *Help me!*

Carlos put out a hand, felt tissue of coldness against his flesh and left it there, in the clutching and desperate fingers of an apparition that shimmered and shook, and again seemed on the verge of winking out.

But where would Mr. Doyle go if he vanished this time?

Pete clenched his teeth. His heart thudded like a hammer on tinplate. He reached down into the deep hole with the spade, trying to keep it from trembling in his hands. Suddenly the sounds he'd heard from within the casket ceased.

Above him, on the ground, the candle flame was extinguished.

"Sweet baby Jesus," the old man prayed in the gathering darkness of the grave, and snapped the catches on the coffin lid with the tip of the spade. *I was imaginin' again,* he told himself, gasping for air as his heartbeat continued to accelerate, telling him that he was wrong and that he should rise from the grave and run. *Just us chickens.*

As he pulled on the coffin lid, using both hands, it began to creak. Tugging mightily, sweat coursing down his leathery face and turning cold on his chest and beneath his collar, he realized that the piercing sound of creaking was increasing in volume, getting louder and louder, like a dissonant chorus of women's voices starting to scream.

And then the lid came free, banged against the wall of the grave as the old man jumped to one side, and the highpitched squeal of the screaming women was drowned out by the panic-stricken shriek of the old man who'd looked directly into the pit of Hell.

A figure rose from the earth, from the casket—and as it kept coming, drawing Old Pete's popeyed gaze of quivering astonishment, it grew, it stretched toward the baleful skies in the midst of a tower of acrid crimson smoke. Pete smelled the terrible odor from the smoke from the lengthening creature, and tasted its rank bitterness in his puckering mouth. Fifteen feet, eighteen, twenty feet and more the hellish being grew, and flung out its massive arms, the clawed nails of its dagger-fingered hands spreading a red, hooded cape the width of the world Pete knew. And then, lowering a face too hideous to register upon the old man's mind in detail, the hellish colossus whipped the cape forward, enveloping Pete in its endless whirls and spirals of flame. "No, please," he cried, although he did not know it; and when the being's laughter began to beat against the distant buildings with the cannonading thunder of gunfire, Old Pete whispered the name of his Savior, slipped from the folds of the voluminous cape, and pitched forward into the open casket.

Newton Link looked down, curious, smiling with pride.

It had been a very long while—*too long*—since he'd been life-side. In the field. Ah, what a mistake it had been to let so much precious time pass him by! Not that he didn't have all the time in the world, the cosmos; but he'd forgotten there was so much *direct*, deep-down satisfaction to taking charge personally, to seeing the last terror in their faces with his own avid eyes.

Promising himself not to wait so long until he left Hell the next time, he allowed himself to shrink to his customary six feet in height. Customary, in any case, in terms of workaday obligations such as crossing swords with that fat fool, Chauncey Wells.

The dead old black lay in the all but empty arms of Zachary Doyle's mortal remains, and Link hesitated when he saw that they both appeared to be smiling. Link laughed, keeping his voice down this time. *Of course, you're smiling,* he reflected, crossing his arms and nudging the aged black with a polished toe. *Death satisfies, doesn't it, gentlemen? Death fits your kind. It's what you live for!*

Straightening his spine, Link raised his left arm and the scarlet cape came to life, fluttering in the hot, all but airless gravesite. At once, both bodies caught fire —an ugly, yellowish, uremic kind of fire—and the soaring flames would have been intolerable for any creature composed of flesh and blood. Licking, lapping, they devoured the flesh in the open coffin without scorching or searing the fabric of the forever-conveyance. When the burning stopped, seeping back into Newton Link's great cape, there wasn't a trace of odor on the still air—and not a trace of Old Pete or Zachary Edson Doyle.

Link applauded his own performance and whirled, striding up the path which a now nonexistent old black had once trod. He could scarcely have been more pleased with himself. He'd been quite sure that Chauncey Wells had seriously considered resurrecting the body of that meaningless wordsmith named Doyle, but Wells could fry in Hell, or do penance on some ludicrous puff of cloud in one of Heaven's back pastures! Because even Wells, as knowledgeable and brilliant as he was, could not return life to a corpse that no longer existed!

Standing beneath the streetlight, consulting a handsome address book drawn from his fine leather attache case, Newton Link might have been a dignified man-about-town—a distinguished businessman, or a film celebrity perhaps, passing through Indianapolis. The red cape, which might have seemed excessive on anyone else, seemed elegant, another mark of his unquestionable class.

He found the name he sought in the book, and the address; and he gave the world of the living his most benefic, utterly devious and evil smile. Only one simple step remained and he would procure not only one reasonably desirable soul for his Chief, but *two* . . .

CHAPTER 24

I held on to the little boy's finger like a drowning man clinging desperately to a stick. I'm sorry to use such a cliche because I know writers are supposed to come up with better, fresher imagery than that.

But as I said earlier, I think, I'm trying here to report the facts as straightforwardly and honestly as possible, under trying circumstances. And when you think you're going to *disappear*, literally—not to die, with the promise of paradise, rest, or plain oblivion in your mind, but literally to be switched out of existence like a light being turned off—you do not work particularly hard at achieving the perfect metaphor, simile, or epigram.

Destruction and chaos have always been anathema to creativity. The best one can do with them, when all the shouting and speech-making is done, is to describe them for that nebulous body of future readers we call "posterity."

You probably wonder what was happening to me, when Carlos pulled out of his own psychic tailspin and had the guts to touch me. Well, so did I, at the time; because I didn't have any idea that an old typewriter-taker and a representative of Hell were using my grave as a battleground. All I can tell you is that there was this first instant, when I felt lightheaded and at the same time strangely violated, or invaded; and then the second moment when there were precisely two things left in the world of the living that I could see: Carlos' bright, haunted, beautiful eyes.

(Now, I guess it's safe to say that the agent from the Underworld wasn't sure himself what would happen after he disinterred my casket, opened it, and climbed inside. Presumably, Link was still after my soul and didn't know that he was taking the chance that neither he nor the heavenly agent would ever be able to claim it. I also do not know, even now, what is so precious about the human spirit or the particular *kind* of soul Heaven and Hell pursue. I don't doubt it, not for a moment; but even for those in what is called After-death, there are cosmic questions to which answers are never presented.)

And so, not knowing even that much about it, I saw Carlos' eyes, felt the marvelous touch of living flesh on mine, and tried to fight against the feeling I had. God, it was *weird!* Because there was no pain, the way there'd been at my mortal death, just . . . a sensation of *unbearable loss.* Of fading away, losing not merely consciousness but all sense of identity and of recollection. That awful second, I could not have told you what "eyes" were, or "fingers," or Carlos, or Louise and Zach Doyle, life or death. I knew I was losing *everything*, and it was easily my most frightening moment, even worse than awakening in my casket.

But once Carlos succeeded in pulling me back, I was all right. An adjustment, I suppose, was made somewhere, either in my own mind, my burning bones in the open grave, or possibly among representatives of Afterdeath ranking far higher than either of the two adversaries. My mind cleared, I was very much "with it," and I sank to the floor more from relief and memory of how I'd felt than from dizziness or ongoing terror.

"You was—evaporating," Carlos said, swallowing hard.

I grinned in relief, released his fingers. Where I'd held them, there was a lightness from psychic pressure and a faint, bluish discoloration as though from frostbite or another sharp coldness.

"Evaporation? Well, that's as good a description of it as any, son," I told him earnestly, surprised by how strong my voice sounded to me, and by the remarkable fact that the other children, Missy and Andy, had *heard* me. Abruptly, I was aware of the anxiety in their faces, and an angry sense of injustice toward a bizarre destiny which left innocent little children exposed to my inexplicable and quite manifest phenomena. How self-centered I'd become! Clearly, I would have to make sure they got home safe and sound (even though I hated parting with my pal Carlos).

But the ever-shifting enigma that was my lot continued to amaze me. When I smiled at Missy and Andy, I found it suddenly easier to sustain an appearance of substance and normality; when I put out my paternal arms, they scurried instantly into them. "Sh-h," I soothed, gently, "everything will be fine."

And that moment it was. Because neither girl nor boy jerked or screamed, or in any fashion pulled away as if suffering from the unnatural coldness I'd exuded. Carlos' eyes met mine, sensing what was happening. Astoundingly, blessedly, it was exactly the way I remembered it feeling when I had held my own son close to my heart without knowing what a privilege it was.

The black child studied my face, which wore, I'm sure, a widening smile. Without warning, he giggled and pointed. "You're lookin' real natural!" he observed.

"It must be the experience I just had," I said wonderingly. "Feeling as if I were disappearing. Evaporating. It must have . . . changed me in some way."

"How do you feel?" he asked, carefully reaching with his arms, touching my cheek with his fingers.

"Great!" I exclaimed. I laughed, stood, hugged the little boy and girl in my arms, adoring their weight, the reality of them, their small hearts beating with excitement. Then an awesome thought crossed my mind and I looked down at Carlos beseechingly, as if he somehow had control of my destiny. "Am I—*alive* again?"

For a moment, he didn't answer. He stared down at his hands, at the fingers which had grazed my cheek. "Most of the cold is gone, but not all of it." He hesitated before looking up at me with anguish in his delicate features. "Mr. Doyle, you aren't *real*—I could put my hand right through you, by pushin'." Tears glistened. "It's like your ectoplasm, or whatever it is, has got all *solid*, or something. I don't think it will— *Hold on!*"

I did, grabing at him, knowing as I stared that he was receiving a message, a communication from somebody other than me. His gaze rose to my face, disturbed. "It's temporary," he said, like a man relaying information gained from a phone call. "Somebody . . . *awful* . . . was in your coffin. He burnt up your body and—*replaced* you for a few minutes." Ruefully, Carlos shook his head. "It ain't gonna last, Mr. Doyle; you'll be like you was in an hour or two."

To conserve my waning strength, I put Andy and Missy back on the floor and then looked across the huge old bedroom where I'd lain, pretending I was asleep. Sleeping the way people, living beings, did. I wanted, then, for all three children to be gone. I'd been right about the way I felt toward those who were alive; they had to be chased off, because all they could do, whatever they intended, was hurt me. The cruelty of what was being done seemed so great, so unfathomable, systematic torture on nearly a Holocaustic level.

But before I could express my bitterly unhappy feelings to Carlos, I saw that he was still listening, gripped, even rapt, at the message being piped from God knew where into his unobstructed and tractable mind. It was getting very late at night and the window at his back displayed an obsidian darkness into which he appeared to merge, all except his knowing eyes, as his intensity increased.

"He says," Carlos whispered, his thoughts more perspicuous and intelligible than his spoken words, "that you still have a chance to go *home*, to go on to Paradise. But it isn't here in this old place, Mr. Doyle, and it will be a whole lot *dangerous* before you find it." Even Andy and Missy were breathless, listening to each syllable uttered by their friend with looks of amazement and awe. "He says, 'There is a *tunnel* at your house—the home of your living past—and it is the one which *everyone* must use . . . to reach the other side. You must go to your house, and find the tunnel.' "

"I can't go back there," I argued, moving my arms sharply in a gesture of dismissal. Already the feeling of relief and ebullience, of good health, was leaving me and I knew I'd be wholly transparent again before long. "I've started a new life here, the best I can."

"You *got* to go back!" Carlos was standing, gesturing to his friends for support. Both the boy and girl nodded, hard. His valor, his concern for me, continued to startle and shame me. "It's your only chance."

"I can't," I snapped, feeling frustration sap my strength as I spoke.

Carlos tugged at my hand. I scarcely felt his touch. "Mr. Doyle, you missus is tryin' to *sell* the house!" he declared, trying to pull me with him. "If she moves away from there you may never see her again!"

I considered. "A tunnel?" I asked, repeating a word of the message given the child. Despite myself, I was slowly following him to the bedroom door. I could see the threadbare carpeting in the corridor, the rich

Oriental rugs which had outlived man and insulted him by seeming deathless. "A tunnel, like the kind mentioned by folks who are dying on the operating table, but come back?"

His head bobbed up and down. I found myself standing in the hallway, bent like an arthritic old codger, looking down at my trio of benefactors and feeling an especially dull ninety-six. Carlos tugged again. "C'mon," he urged me. "We'll walk you home."

"All right." I sighed as I gave up, or relented. "But all three of you have to promise me that you'll go home, too. Okay?"

They exchanged glances. Carlos grinned as he led the way toward the crumbling steps of the mansion. "We'll go home," he promised. "Just as soon as you do."

I shuffled my way downstairs, through the living room, and outside. It seemed to me one hundred years since I'd last left the house, and the small pleasure of looking at the moon and stars blended with the first optimism I'd had in a long time.

I guess I was still too self-centered to realize, until later, that my friend Carlos had tears in his eyes.

After the aged black junkman had accepted the information about Zach's grave and departed, Louise closed the door and leaned against it wearily on her pressing palms. The late winter night rain had a chill to it that she could sense through the door and she shuddered the length of her body.

It seemed to her she had been cold forever. Now it

was the icy rain, before that the ceaseless snow, and the period of striving to adjust to Zach's absence; and before that, his unexpected death and burial, the coldest time of all.

But the impression of having been quick-frozen, like a popsicle, or cryogenically sustained—of being frigidly deadened yet obliged to go through all the little formalities of a living person—did not go away. It kept gathering inside her, it built ice castles around her heart, walls of glacial stoicism which rose higher and higher, until one's feeling of living warmth could no longer grope around the edges.

A woman took the risk, when there was love and she opened herself up to the kind of absorbing relationship she'd had with Zachary Doyle, of encouraging a situation which did not truly end at the grave. Mildly, she regretted not having known how much she loved him when there was still time, but Louise wasn't given to many moods of second guessing. She also did not resent marrying him, but she saw, nonetheless, that for the victim as well as the survivor, death ended little if anything. It just went on happening, like a lovely flower planted upside down, forced to grow secretly in the stifling darkness.

A widow's roots were exposed and the seed itself, if one could not find a means of diverting it, sooner or later was lost in the tough, relentless weeds of pointless survival.

Shaking off her feelings, she moved deeper into the house. The friendly old man was either superstitious or mad. Zach was not, *people* were not, earthbound after dying. Instead of worrying about his soul, she needed to be her practical self and worry about her own health for a change. Determinedly, she went upstairs, filled the tub, and undressed. Perhaps the hot water would prove soothing. Perhaps its warm encouragement would endure.

Perhaps she could sleep, finally, without awaking to creaking sounds in the house.

When she was naked and had one foot raised to step into the tub, however, she froze that way and felt a freezing shiver dart and dip into every crevice of her body. It was absurd, of course—

But *someone* was watching her. The unpleasant sensation of *eyes*, caressing every curve, was unmistakable.

Ordinarily, since she'd never been a neurotic person, she might simply have laughed at the feeling and taken her bath.

But whether it was the old man's mildly frightening request, to know where Zach was, or the pent-up loneliness and despair of the months without her husband —or *something else*—her matter-of-fact mind could not decide.

The bathroom door, ajar, *moved*—or appeared to. The light in the hallway seemed to glare, as if blinding her to what was out there.

The curtains at the bathroom window were billowing, pregnant with a breeze she could not feel— would something fall from them? Increasingly frightened, Louise turned her head, just faintly, at the noise from the wash basin.

Drip. *Pause*. Drip. Drip. *Pause*. Drip. The faucet, apparently in a fashion that was calculated and determined, was leaking, and it hadn't done that since Zach put in new washers, a year and a half ago. From where she stood, knee bent, poised above the tub, she waited for the next drop and it did not come again for an eternity. *Drip*, it finally said. Staring at it, heartbeat accelerating, she waited for the distinct pause, and for the second, slightly offkey drip.

But it had stopped. Louise shut her eyes, dizzy; opened them, looked down at her bathwater.

A roach nearly two inches long was swimming upstream, perching on her washcloth and wriggling its antennae.

Her shriek, and the other sound she made when she fell back from the bathtub against the tiled wall, were momentarily adequate to smother the *third* noise.

But only for a moment.

Someone was knocking downstairs at the front door. And her waterproof Timex indicated it was nearly midnight.

Wobbly and breathless, partly worried by who was rapping at such an hour and half glad for human company, Louise thrust her arms into a woolly white robe and quickly padded barefoot into the hall. Maybe it was the old man, Pete, come back for further information.

"It's duck-weather out here!" called a muffled voice, and the knocking resumed with urgency. "C'mon, open the door, Louise! It's me!"

She reached the foot of the stairs and hurried toward the door, surprised. Because she hadn't anticipated seeing the lanky lawyer again unless it was on business. Distant thunder boomed and lightning crackled at the bay window like something frying.

"Hullo, stranger," she said in greeting, throwing the door wide and smiling.

But his tall, lean form was pushing past her and making for the kitchen. She only caught a glimpse of him but he wasn't wearing his glasses, and something else seemed out of place to her. "I left something here," he called over his shoulder. "I won't be a moment."

Bewildered, holding her robe together and slowly shuffling after him, Louise saw Mike tug open the basement door. "What did you forget?" she inquired, plagued by what seemed wrong and also becoming miffed. This had better be damnably important if he thought he had the right to visit her whenever he chose! His footsteps clattered down the steps and she slipped into the doorway, peering into the depths of gloom. She repeated, with much less good humor, "I said, *Michael*, what did you *forget?*"

"Oh, nothing much," came his voice. He was moving with uncharacteristic swiftness around the basement, occasionally making a racket when he bumped into things. Why hadn't he turned on the light? "Shit," he swore mildly. "Maybe you can lend me a hand?"

Louise paused, shivering. It was cold at the top of the steps and the floor was like ice beneath her bare feet. "All right," she agreed at last, sighing. She turned on the lights and ventured out upon the short landing. One or two of the steps, she knew, were rotting. Cautious, she gripped the banister to descend. "What did you say you forgot?"

"Didn't say," came the muffled reply. She could see him now, his back to her, standing against the wall, near the furnace. He seemed to be rubbing his hands together, and that was when she understood what had seemed out of place about him: he'd complained about the rain, but his clothing was absolutely *dry*. And why in hell was he wearing a cape? "But," he added, "I will . . ."

He turned to look up at her, but not with Mike Abernethy's lantern-jawed features. Instead, it was the face of a fiend.

"I forgot," he said softly, reaching for her nearest ankle, *"your soul."*

CHAPTER 25

Sometimes when we come upon something that suddenly is more frightening than we can bear, we turn away from it and do our best to pretend we simply didn't see it.

And so Louise Doyle spun away from the unsurpassably terrifying face which had leered up at her from the basement—whirled to get away, darted toward the door through which she had so recently passed. The movement was instinctive, an automatic motion of urgent self-survival.

But it did not catch the devil at the foot of the steps offguard.

She did not see what it was he did with his eyes, his mind, to make it happen. But before she could even touch the basement door, it slammed shut with the ringing finality of an airless vault door, openable again only by virtue of a timelock, or a miracle. The vibration from the deafening shock of the slamming door quivered on the air almost palpably, like a violin string freshly plucked from the moist inner portions of a dead cat, with traces of shredded fur and sundered flesh attached to it still, and dripping.

For several pounding seconds Louise braced her arms against the door, leaning on her hands, striving to think and trying to excise from her memory those features at which she had looked. Because she'd always been a sensible woman, a practical person, she knew perfectly well what her senses told her and did not even try to open the door. She just bowed her head, tried to *think*.

And for the same reason, too, she knew that what she had seen was not imagination. That there was no point in pretending to herself thta she had *not* seen the being whose name she did not know in his original form. And when she turned back, as she understood she must, she also knew that the beast from Hell would still be there.

"Louise . . . *dear.*"

She clawed the sealed door with her nails from several inches above her head to a point even with her bosom, then frantically drew her robe together, there and below. Her feet, she realized as her flesh crawled, were bare; her naked legs were well above his—*its*—eye-level, and she felt her buttocks flinch from the probing gaze drifting thoughtfully over her body. She nuzzled her chin down into her breast and pressed her forehead against the basement door, shaking her head faintly, squeezing her long legs together tightly. *Had he moved, had he come closer?*

It wasn't Mike Abernethy's voice he was imitating now, mocking; probably it wasn't his own, either, since she didn't doubt that he was the champion of thieves and, while she did not wonder how she knew *what* he was, she knew that too—and a being who would steal souls would certainly take the voice of a charming, attractive man. Take and pervert it, as he had done, into the most honeyed, sweetly-inflected, gently-confident, alluringly-seductive, sinister and *sepulchral* voice she'd ever heard. It was a voice that knew everything about her, all the small and petty secrets every human being possesses, all the dreadful things she dared not even confide openly to herself, and from which she fled whenever the sunshine of truth or love once more warmed her spirit.

Realizing that, understanding he had already poked and clawed inside her mind, her soul, everything except for her mortal flesh, she knew why he had looked the way he had, and slowly, almost curiously, made herself turn upon the dim landing above the basement steps to peer down through the shadows at him.

Without his bag of Mephistophalean tricks—without melodramatically soaring many meters above the frigid floor; without displaying the afterdeath demeanor of an aged soul that had feasted upon succulent evil—Newton Link was the *other side* of handsome. Instead of staring into a face with enraged eyes and a gaping hell-hole of a mouth ringed by white fangs, Louise saw a second time the much more terrifying face of an ideal and beautiful man whose love and total regard had been kept exclusively for himself, and whose humanity had stopped at the instant he turned from the mirror of vanity. The abandoned gift of handsomeness, the shock of seeing all that Link had lost, were what made it the face of a fiend.

But she saw in detail, as well, what had happened to those flawless features even before his death, centuries ago. The classic, wide and high forehead, now bore a single, querulous line that would, with rancor, enhance the ferocity of a self-serving frown. The acquiline, elegant nose seemed somewhat pointed, because the upper lip had sneered too often and sank into the hollow of perpetual sulk. The full, symmetrical mouth, giver of so many passionately deceitful kisses that the lower lip pouted and drooped, was petulant and epicene and mottled by a faint, scarlet bruise. A square, manly chin, fixed and humorless as granite; athletic shoulders, jauntiness become strut; a mane of glossy, shining, luxuriant black hair riddled with random strands that bristled porcinely and were yellow as bile. A torso that had been sleek-muscled and vibrant, turned to inflexible stone; and legs once lively and nimble gone to a slight stoop at the knee, as if avid to spring.

Louise gaped at the well-formed head once again and pressed fingertips to her lips as sick revulsion rose inside. Rounded, pale-skinned, oddly glistening, it was less a head than an *ornament*, a bauble one might hang upon a Christmas tree until she perceived that, like the eyes in certain paintings, it *followed* her wherever she went with the lurid sheen of lust like ice.

Once caught in the dull glow of the recessed black eyes, however, she saw with real astonishment that the ruined old devil was *crying*. The impression was unmistakable, undeniable; there were soft tears forming and framed by the impossibly long, curling lashes, as though something about her, some essentially *good* thing that was most woman, most fully feminine of all, had penetrated Link to the nucleus of what he'd been a long while ago and *touched* him—drawn up from him a tenderness, a yieldingness, a nurturable sweetness of spirit that he had longed to feel again, and share only with her. Gently, he raised his hand, put out his arm slowly and carefully toward her, the manicured fingernails polished until they shone. Affectionately, discreetly, he smiled, and the neatly trimmed, boyish mustache he affected smiled along. Lovingly, the tears in his great, luxuriously shimmering eyes fell upon his wan cheeks and one—one tear only—dropped upon the hem of her robe. "*You,*" he said in the throbbing baritone voice which knew her so well, which accepted her totally for everything she was . . . "*Always, it is you.*"

Louise choked back a sob and lifted a trembling hand, ready to embrace him.

Then she saw the grotesque, tumescence pressing against the front of Link's trousers and her nostrils caught, for the first time, the stink of burning sulphur rising almost tangibly from his crouched and ancient form.

"*No!*" she shouted, even as the terror regrouped

within her and attacked all her senses, dizzying her.

Enraged, Newton Link temporarily allowed his psychic mask to drop, and the creature he had become after centuries of service to a master who approved of emulation was exposed to Louise in a revolting flash.

She saw squirming things in the sockets of his burning eyes; encrusted wetness, with tiny legs that moved, in nostrils the size of a fist—and a toothless mouth that stretched wide like pocked and lecherous labia over an organ breathing golden flame from a million miles away. She heard the sounds of agonized multitudes in a chorus of pain that had begun an infinity ago.

And then she heard nothing more.

He caught her easily, stretched her on the dusty table against the wall. He cursed—expertly, self-indulgently, directing it at himself. For an instant Link believed she was dead, and that would not do at all; it was much too soon for that. Somehow, for him, they were never quite the tasty morsels in afterdeath that they were before. Something went out of them; something was lost.

He stood at the side of the table, looking down at her. Matters had gone exceedingly well until now. The spirit of Zachary Doyle would be on his way, and before long the victory would belong to Link's side, not Wells'. A victory that fat, angelic fool had not envisioned, since *two* souls would be claimed! But the woman had fainted, and he'd wanted her to scream when Doyle arrived—beg for her life, her soul, so that the male spirit would unhesitatingly descend to this symbolic replica of Hell.

Link smiled, reached. Perhaps she would awaken

after he'd begun; they usually did, but whether it was from pain, terror, or some knowing sickness of the soul, he'd never figured out. No matter.

Despite his experience, his fingers fumbled when he began opening her robe. Silently, he cursed his nervousness, his ridiculous, schoolboy craving. She was so beautiful, so utterly helpless in his hands, and he had such plans for her. What he could not manage physically, he would easily direct with his mind. Link smiled, his black eyes glittering, and momentarily rubbed his hands together. If she was cooperative, he might even give her the command to enjoy it! Licking his lips, dry but for the saliva of lust rising inside him, his curving, clawed fingers reached down as he knelt.

The door at the front of the house opened with a crash.

Furious, frustrated, Newton Link closed his eyes and ordered himself to become calm. There'd be another occasion, another opportunity—there always was, there always would be. Now he had to lure the male spirit into the basement with him.

But when he turned toward the basement steps, Link paused, mildly alarmed.

There were *other* steps in the house, besides those of Zachary Doyle. Lighter ones. Three sets of them.

Well, isn't that wonderful! Link thought, chuckling to himself. *Volunteers!*

"Why have you stopped out there?"

Carlos, holding the other two children back with raised arms and spreading fingers, looked up at the ghost. Mr. Doyle was inside his house already, still solid and substantial enough for anyone to see him. But that wasn't the problem.

"I was wrong," Carlos said firmly, bobbing his chin and gesturing. "C'mon, Mr. Doyle, we don't belong in there after all."

The spirit frowned. "What are you talking about?" he demanded.

Carlos swallowed. "This building's full of *wickedness*," he replied at last. "*The worst.*" Carlos stopped talking, unable to find the words for it. He felt Andy and Missy, beside him, staring at him and getting more spooked by the moment, but he couldn't help it. He knew what he sensed. "There's *evil* here, Mr. Doyle, from Hell itself. I can't stop it. And neither can you."

The ghost turned his head, looking into the home that had been his, *feeling* what lay in waiting. Profiled in the doorway with the street light's reflection illuminating his transiently-seen features, Doyle reminded Carlos of faded watercolor paintings he'd seen. This was costing the spirit everything he had; Carlos didn't think he could remain visible much longer. But the answer from the apparition entered Carlos' thoughts: "Louise is here. She *needs* me."

Before the small boy could respond, Mr. Doyle was rushing into the house, looking in every direction.

And a high, woman's voice was calling, eerily, from somewhere below, "Zach—I'm here! In the basement."

Seeing no one, scared out of his wits, Andy whirled and began running, tugging his little sister after him. Startled, Carlos glanced at them as they flashed down the walk and out of sight, chunky little Andy calling after him, "I'm too *cold* to stay!"

Smiling but wary, Carlos followed the ghost into the house and discovered Mr. Doyle standing, his entire form outlined by wavering lines, before the basement door. The boy started to speak and then *saw*, in his mind's eye, what waited behind the door.

Before he could stop him, the spirit, using his temporary substantiality, was ripping the door open, revealing a sight the boy had feared he would never see again. Laughing, running forward with total abandon, Carlos was joyous beyond his wildest dreams!

His Gramp—Old Pete—stood in the basement entrance holding an unconscious white woman in arms that fluctuated from visibility to nothingness in just the same way Mr. Doyle's did.

He did not appear to see Carlos. The old eyes, all that were still bright about him, were intently fixed upon the spirit of Zachary Doyle—enigmatic, all-knowing.

But what Carlos saw *behind* the shade of his beloved grandfather—a moving miasma of crimson smoke, in the midst of it a being which clawed at Gramp's broad back, spewing torrents of filth, too livid with mad ire even to do the things of which he was hideously capable—nearly made the child's eyes pop out.

"Take her and run, Mr. Doyle." The words—Gramps' voice, heard only by Carlos and the ghost in their respective minds—were filled with grief. *"Take your missus to Paradise—now!"*

Carlos watched wonderingly. The spectral Doyle

took Louise into his arms. His gaze, locked with Gramp's, said much more than the few words he mustered. "Sir . . . thank you."

Old Pete nodded—and was divided in two from head to crotch by the swift, cleaving, crimson arm of the monster behind him, the devil who had summoned them in Louise's voice. "How many times must I *kill you!*" it roared as the old man's shade turned to ash and was scattered in directions beyond enumeration by a blast of searing flame.

Zach gasped. Louise's eyes were opening; she was still alive! Wildly, indecisively, he glanced at the terrible creature emerging from the basement doorway. Then he pressed his wife against his momentarily substantial chest and ran toward the front of the house.

The front door slammed shut; the house fell uncannily silent; and a brave small boy remained behind to confront a devil from Hell.

CHAPTER 26

Hugging Louise's semi-conscious body against me, I ran frantically toward the front door of my house. I didn't want to leave poor little Carlos behind; he was the only friend I'd made since dying, and I loved him. But I simply could not think of anything else to do, not then. Events were happening with such rapidity—fantastic and frightening things I had never truly believed possible when I was a living man—that it was quite beyond me to think clearly.

But what galvanized me to any kind of action was realizing my Louise *lived*. When I saw her first in Old Pete's arms, I'd known at once that he was dead, a spirit like me. I suppose like does respond to like. And spirits, despite my own shock-endowed imitation of life, could not ordinarily move or grasp the so-called "real" objects, except by the force of the mind. It did not occur to me then that the fine old fellow had spent eighty years preparing for this, in a way; that he'd looked forward to the afterdeath, or that he'd always possessed gifts far greater than those I had acquired since my own demise. And so, the moment her dear form was thrust into my arms, I assumed Louise had been killed by the devil behind Pete and that the old man's actions were nothing more than a gallant and compassionate gesture—and that, already feeling my corporality ebbing away from me, I would not for long be able to hold her body.

The instant I saw those beautiful and vital eyes looking up, trying to focus, I simply remembered what I'd always believed. That my first responsibility was to the woman I loved and everything else—every*one* else—was secondary.

All this, I'm sure you realize, was going on at an unreal, frenetic pace, including the running I did toward the door. We must have been a strange sight. I mentioned the fantastic quality of what was happening, but you really cannot understand how pervasive and inescapable it was. Don't forget I'd been out of the flesh for a considerable time. Back in the depressing, lonely mansion, when my temporary condition of materiality began, I'd felt heavy, gross and awkward, even oddly burdened by the psychic impression of having flesh and bone. Now, pressing a living body to my chest and willing my legs to run, I did not have any longer the effortless *glide* I'd experienced for weeks. Instead, I was weighty, ponderous and intolerably inept.

Once outside, slamming the door behind us (as if it could possibly restrain the basement monster!) I shivered as night air ruffled my hair and played on my momentary face and hands. While I knew we were still in immense danger, when I saw the trees in my yard swaying soundlessly, as graceful as dark ballerinas moved by music only they could hear, I stroked Louise's hair and tried to memorize that beauty I'd taken for granted. We shared the same stirring wind, the trees and Louise and I; we came from the same earth, and always our roots reached down into it. She had shut her eyes once more but I felt her heart beating, a thready and uncertain throb that told me she'd taken all she could handle.

But where, I wondered with a fresh flush of panic, could we go? To Paradise, the old man had commanded. But *how?*

Carlos' thoughts filled my mind, replacing the terror with his springtime warmth: *"The garage,"* he cried, as resonantly as if he'd stood at my side and spoken with his engaging, highpitched voice—*"run for your den!"*

Again I was driven—compelled—to hurry. Getting a good grip on my wife, I whirled, saw the garage, and lumbered over to the driveway with as much speed and alacrity as I could generate. What moonlight there was told me, when I happened to see my wrists and hands, that I was beginning to wink out; yet I knew that if I failed to reach shelter, the result would be Louise's death and God knew what to our immortal souls. "Take the high ground!" they'd ordered, in old war films; but both Louise and I had chuckled at the way heroines in horror movies always managed to get themselves trapped in attics or hay-lofts.

Yet it did not occur to me to question my friend Carlos' command. If he could still think of Louise and me when he faced such hideous, personal peril—if he had that much presence of mind, and if the little boy cared *that much*—any other choice would be a betrayal. I even felt a brilliant surge of hope; I knew, somehow, that the fundamental goodness of our cause would win out. Hadn't we always been promised as much?

Then I glanced back at the house as we started to enter the garage, and I felt my emotions of optimism turn to tatters, and everything I'd ever believed in was shredded like confetti.

The house—our home, our place was ablaze. Not with fire, because earth-side flames have a distinctive look to them one never quite forgets. It was an outpouring of absolute detestation, a flood of Hell-born fury; it was an under-earth inferno struggling to get out, a soul-shriveling explosion of lusting redness, and each unnatural, lapping tongue was outlined by a sallow yellowness of despair, the color of pus, or killing jaundice. I saw the liverish blaze lie against our windows like a series of pawing, imbecilic hands trying to push away the panes and reach for us, to drag us down to the hideous flames that had been burning, I realized, since Time began.

I half-stumbled into the garage and saw a bundle of furry *something* rise from the dark corner—Angelo, our dog, barking in a queer mixture of joy at seeing us, and some second emotion that gave his welcoming woofs an un-St. Bernard-like yelp. I'd have sworn, then, that Angelo somehow knew what was happening; and when I started up the stairs toward the door to my beloved old workshop, Angelo followed us more nimbly than he'd ever traveled a flight of steps before.

Could Carlos be right? I wondered, utterly exhausted, my strength swiftly waning and my own feeble light flickering as if I had batteries dying inside. *Will going into my den save us?* Balancing Louise just so, I put out my pale hand to reach for the doorknob—

And a scream of unbearable pain sounded in both my mind and my ears. Half falling against the door, I could scarcely stand it myself; because it was *Carlos'* shriek, *Carlos'* agony, and I thought I knew what had happened.

"*Zach.*" Louise, eyes open, was staring at me with the expression of fear that I'd never wished to see. I felt her heart leap against my chest; I tried to find words to tell her it was all right, that she needn't be frightened —not of *me!* But the terror was there, it had all been too much.

And when her eyes rolled back, then closed, I knew that my wife was gone.

That evil, and ignorance, and fear had won again, and I'd lost my final hope for any happiness at all.

The pots and pans rose from the sink where they'd been drying, sped unerringly through the redly-hazy air, and battered Newton Link's upraised arms. When he brushed them aside and stalked into the kitchen after the boy, a broom batted at his ankles, trying to trip him. He moved forward irresistibly, the handle of the broom snapping.

He said something to Carlos then for the first time, but it wasn't the first time Carlos had ever heard those particular words. They didn't surprise him. He'd supposed their original source was an evil entity just like this one.

Agile, blessed by the energy of youth, Carlos danced nimbly away from the advancing Link, staying on his toes and moving like a miniature boxer. He was too filled with a sense of injustice to be as terrified as perhaps he should have been. He'd seen what the old devil had done to Gramp, and he was protected not only by his boy's quickness and his inherited gift of psychokinesis but by the love he'd always feel for his grandfather.

"C'mon," he taunted the implacable creature, and backed toward the sink. His fists moved rapidly, constantly; once he even jabbed with his left, the way he'd seen Sugar Ray Leonard do it, and almost grazed Link's jaw. "C'mon and get me!"

Instantly Link raised his right hand and his voluminous cape swept up from the floor to halt Carlos' sudden intention to dart into the dining room. Link saw the look of amazement in the bright brown eyes; he realized that the aggressive youngster had just understood the truth—that he knew every thought in the child's mind the second it occurred.

And he grew bored with the ludicrous contest since the boy refused even to react with the fright Link wished to see. What was the matter with these fools?

How *dare* they defy him? But there was the question of the fleeing spirit and the woman. To stop their escape, he'd have to finish this dark-skinned mortal quickly and transport himself to the garage. Not that there was a problem, certainly; he could easily—

There was an incredible instant when contact with the child's mind was broken, and Link barely had time to realize it.

Blocking Link's probe as he had his grandfather's, Carlos was seizing the hose from the sink and turning on the hot water, then spraying it upon the being before him, watching it become hotter, joyously seeing it turn to *scalding* water, full in the devil's face!

Laughing, Carlos danced away from the sink, moving agilely toward the dining room door, still training the streaming hose in Link's direction.

Then he stopped, frozen in his tracks, as the mustached face leaned back as if *revelling* in the scalding stream. "Thank you," Link whispered, "that's very refreshing . . ."

Carlos dropped the hose as the red, dripping face above him began to *change*.

To *grow*.

Carlos tried to move, then; couldn't. He no longer had control of his muscles. He tried to shout, as the laughing mouth before him grew, widened, the razorish fangs becoming inches long, but the devil no longer even wished to hear his screams. When the mouth was larger than his own head, still spreading wider, Carlos closed his eyes and remembered the prayers Momma had taught him.

There was a feeling of moistness all around his head,

the worst stink Carlos had ever smelled, a sensation of his neck being pricked in a hundred painful places—
And then, he was permitted to scream.
Once.

CHAPTER 27

How very often, in most of our lives, we top all that other nonsense we've been sending into the atmosphere by boldly declaring that things couldn't possibly be worse! A job full of boring details or dissension is taken away from us, perhaps unfairly; a relationship which never fulfilled its bright promise collapses; the check doesn't arrive on time, or the cat dies, or your in-laws accuse you of being a heartless turkey—and that's when we put on our big, brave smiles, shrug, and coolly defy all those frightful forces beyond human control: "Well, it's happened; the axe has fallen. At least, it's over. Now nothing truly terrible can ever happen again and I'm shock-proof!"

I'd thought the same things thousands of times before dying, and a hundred times after. When I regained consciousness in my coffin but couldn't get out. When my own dog didn't see me. When I was full of self-pity and left my house.

Now I knew how foolish I'd been. I knew worse things *could* happen.

Because I had to watch my dead wife's pretty head fall back into the crook of my elbow, the vivid color flee her cheeks, and see that altogether heartbreaking, numbing stare of sightless eyes which once had danced with brilliant life.

So I just sort of stood there before the door to my empty den in the garage with Louise close to me and no idea what I should do, and somehow I couldn't put her down. I suppose I wanted simply to go on standing there, crying like a little kid, till the end of time. There'd never been an anguish as deep as mine then, but I won't try to describe it. I couldn't possibly. All I understood was that whatever strands of hope I'd been clinging to had just come unraveled between my fingers and vanished into nothingness, as I would myself in a matter of moments. Like everything else I could remember, the notion of finding sanctuary in my silly writer's den had been a waste of time and passion.

How stupid, how idiotic, could a man get, dead or alive? Hell! Even if my study hadn't been cleaned out long ago by Old Pete, Orville and little Carlos—if it had been left furnished, if it had remained the way it was when my "sick spell" came upon me and stayed forever—what could I have done against that creature in my basement? Thrown paper wads from the wastebasket at him? Pelted him with old typewriter ribbons and burnt-out Bic lighters? Clobbered him with my desk chair, then stapled him to the wall?

I glanced back down the steps, over the head of faithful Angelo, who was nuzzling Louise's hand with a poignantly curious expression in his soulful eyes, and I saw that the illumination from our house now extended to the garage. It wasn't bright, or alarming in itself; the monster that had surely killed poor Carlos no doubt had gained control of itself and probably had no desire to arouse the entire neighborhood. But the light told me, without a doubt, that it was coming.

Well, let it, I thought, surprising myself. I'd done nothing bad enough to deserve the flames of Hell, and Louise certainly hadn't. I'd spent most of my life feeling guilty about this, responsible for that, as I knew most men did. The majority of people I'd known weren't bad enough, in my opinion, for what a creature like this had in mind. Sure, they passed the buck, tried to think of themselves as the good guys; they put the best possible face on situations they got themselves into.

But Louise hadn't even been guilty of that. Unlike creative types like me, she had been far too practical and direct to make up alibis. She didn't even have the self-serving ability to hide from her own faults and discover those wonderfully ingenious ways in which blame can be pinned on somebody else!

She wasn't, I supposed, perfect. No one was; that's what everybody said, anyway. But I realized then that my love made it impossible for me to see her faults clearly, the way I did so easily with other people. Or putting it in another fashion, those faults of character or personality which ostensibly kept Louise from being a perfect human being were always the kind I could handle, the kind that were fully acceptable to me. And maybe that, when you got down to it, was what love happened to be.

I peered into her quiet face and tears started in my eyes. The most wonderful thing of all about her was that she'd known well the small deceits, the little underhanded things I'd done; the petty furies which sometimes had possessed me, the moments I'd grown so unhappy and frustrated that I'd put myself ahead of everyone and everything with a selfishness that approached egomania—but she had still forgiven me, she'd still loved me!

I thought that was amazing. I thought that entitled her to happiness, at last, and peace. And because there was nothing else I could think to do, I began anew the prayer I'd started once before. A prayer for Louise, who deserved it.

Yes, I know. They say there's no one there to hear me. But somehwere on the fringes of my mind I figured it out this way: if there were such beings as the monstrosity which pursued us—if a man looked around in bewilderment, trying to explain the vicious, brutal, horrifying things that were happening in our society and could find no reason beyond the existence of evil, then it followed that God *is*. Because in a universe of opposites, there *had* to be a source of gentleness, compassion, and love, just as my little friend Carlos had lived his life; the existence of *good* became no longer a matter of belief or blind faith, but a matter of logic.

And of the common sense my wife had quietly and peaceably accepted as her way, and which she'd always believed lay near the core of life.

The door to my den was ajar and, while I was praying, Angelo got to his shaggy feet and began sniffing at it. He was a distraction and I glared at him, trying to sustain the sincerity and continuity of what I was saying. He ignored me, putting his big head against the door and shoving. I started to call his name, but stopped, staring straight ahead.

At first, there was a brilliant white light, formless and almost blinding. It flooded my den, like multiple suns rising upon a distant planet; and there was a warmth to it that made me remember how cold I felt, inside and out. I raised one hand, cupping it to shield my eyes as my lumpy old St. Bernard pushed the door wide.

Before I could stop him, Angelo, his tongue lolling affably and his hindquarters twitching in that amiably curious fashion of his, was through the door.

And *gone*.

Prayer mostly finished, I stared into the whiteness wonderingly and couldn't see Angelo anywhere. For reasons I cannot explain, I didn't feel threatened, nor did I wonder if something were on fire, or if Louise might have put a floodlight in the old den as a warning to prowlers and Angelo had tripped the wire. Actually, I think, some of my senses were numbed by the calm, cascading flood of light, perhaps the very ones which had formerly told my brain that it should be afraid.

Then the white light soundlessly narrowed, became a beam, as if the walls of my old study had somehow contracted.

But the wall farthest from where I stood was no longer there, and the beam of illumination *just kept going*—it plunged straight ahead into unimaginable distances, toward unguessable horizons that seemed to me always to be retreating. To . . . infinity.

"The *tunnel*," I whispered.

I heard old Angelo's best bark from somewhere in the light, good-humored, playful, and frolicking gee-this-is-fun-I-*like*-you bark which told me he was bounding up and down in canine exuberance, romping like a goofy kid in a place that was safe. But I couldn't see him.

I believe there was someone, or something, on the landing behind Louise and me at that moment—a body, or a force that hated, yearned to destroy, and to claim. I had the impression of a darkness so impenetrable that it was like some collapsed, crushing star on which no one could move, or breathe. But I didn't turn back, and the force did not dare go forward. Pressing my wife's face into my shoulder, I followed the light.

Behind me, once we were inside, the study door slammed shut—and disappeared.

For an instant I couldn't move. We seemed to be on a threshold, the illumination faint beneath my feet, the warmth soothing, summoning. It was still somewhat hard to see but I squinted hard and made out the blurred figure of my dog bounding between two figures in shadow. It wasn't possible to go back; the door no longer existed. Moving slowly, cautiously, aware of an obligation to protect my wife's body, I edged forward.

The brilliance of the light dimmed, or perhaps my vision adjusted to it. I knew somehow that we were on the outer limit of the threshold. I could see Angelo vividly, see the backs of the two people playing with him. One belonged to a rather tall man, the other to a smaller person.

They turned to me, smiling, and I found myself making noises of joy and unparalleled relief. "C'mon, Mr. Doyle," cried my friend Carlos, his beautiful eyes brighter than ever. He rumbled Angelo's head and put out his hand, motioning to me. "Just a few steps more!"

The man had something in his arms. He gave me a shy grin. "Your typewriter's waitin' for you," Old Pete called, holding it so I could see it. "I reckon some folks *live* stories instead of tellin' them."

Exulting, I ran toward them, awkwardly, bathed by the remarkable light.

And, "Put me down, silly," ordered my wife, squirming, smiling, starting to laugh. "I can walk."

I looked speechlessly at her and thought she had never seemed more vibrantly alive, more beautiful or dear. When we embraced, it was truly Louise whom I held in my arms, and I knew instantly that she felt my touch, and responded to the kisses I showered on her upturned face.

There was more than light behind Carlos and Old

Pete when, holding hands, we turned to join them. Much more. I caught a glimpse of a clear, azure sky above rolling fields in which a variety of animals lazed, peacefully feeding. I perceived a multitude of shining, endlessly fascinating buildings, unsurpassingly beautiful in their varied design.

I saw clean, white boulevards lined by trees of every kind; the clearest lake I'd ever seen; the houses—*homes*, I felt—of every size and manner of construction.

Then I saw the people. People, yes. Men and women and children whose only differences I could detect from those I'd known in life were in the individual range of consuming interest and a certain unruffled composure—not the bland, bored-and-boring expression of the docile or mindless, but the unthreatened and unthreatening poise of people who did what they wished, and better than they had ever done it before.

"I want to write it down," I whispered, and Old Pete, grinning, returned my typewriter to me.

"Later," Louise said, kissing my cheek and tugging at my arm.

I looked into her laughing eyes. "Later," I agreed.

"C'mon!" called Carlos, racing ahead with Angelo at his heels. Ahead of them, a man I'd never seen reached out to hug the child. Carlos hugged back. "I want you to meet somebody."

He was a very fat man with that rare mixture of dignity and humor, each of them about to boil over. I could tell that immediately. He reminded me, as our hands clasped, of a cross between Sir Winston

Churchill and the actor John Houseman. He looked tired, but happy. "Don't I know you from somewhere?" I asked.

PREFERRED CUSTOMERS!

Leisure Books and Love Spell proudly present a brand-new catalogue and a TOLL-FREE NUMBER

STARTING JUNE 1, 1995
CALL 1-800-481-9191
between 2:00 and 10:00 p.m.
(Eastern Time)
Monday Through Friday

GET A FREE CATALOGUE
AND ORDER BOOKS USING
VISA AND MASTERCARD

LEISURE BOOKS   **LOVE SPELL**